FORT WORTH LIBRARY

⟨☞⟩ **W9-API-320**

## "We can't stop looking. What if—"

"Kylie, it's okay." Nick slipped his strong arm around her.

Instinct warned her not to get too close to this man. Years ago she'd learned what losing him could do to her heart. She couldn't go down that path again. Still, it felt good to be in his arms again.

A shiver skidded over her at the thought of suspending the search. The killer's phone call had directed her here.

"Come on." She grabbed his hand.

The flashlight cast distorted shadows over the barn. They pushed aside cobwebs and searched till they found a box.

Blood pounded in Kylie's ears. She tried not to jump, tried not to breathe as Nick opened the flaps and withdrew a bulging folder. Dozens of roughly cut-out newspaper articles and photos scattered onto the floor.

Her body went rigid when she realized she was looking at articles she'd written, along with black-and-white prints of *herself.* Was she the next victim?

## ANNSLEE URBAN

grew up watching old-time romance movies, to which she attributes her passion for sweet romance, true love and happy endings. A daydreamer at heart, Annslee began her writing journey when the youngest of her five children started school. For several years she worked as a freelance writer for newspapers in her community and has written for magazines and online publications.

Raised in the foothills of Arizona, she survived temperature shock when she moved to Western Pennsylvania, before settling in North Carolina with her husband and children. Aside from writing, Annslee works part-time as a registered nurse in the behavioral health field. She is a member of ACFW, and has served on the board of Carolina Christian Writers.

When she isn't writing, Annslee enjoys cooking, traveling to faraway places, playing with grandbabies and all things chocolate!

You can reach Annslee at
maryannsleeurban@gmail.com,
maryurban.blogspot.com,
facebook.com/mary.a.urban.9.

# SMOKY MOUNTAIN INVESTIGATION

## ANNSLEE URBAN

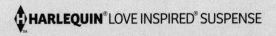

**HARLEQUIN**® LOVE INSPIRED® SUSPENSE

If you purchased this book without a cover you should be aware
that this book is stolen property. It was reported as "unsold and
destroyed" to the publisher, and neither the author nor the
publisher has received any payment for this "stripped book."

LOVE INSPIRED BOOKS

Recycling programs
for this product may
not exist in your area.

PLEASE RECYCLE
THIS PRODUCT IS RECYCLABLE

ISBN-13: 978-0-373-67622-4

SMOKY MOUNTAIN INVESTIGATION

Copyright © 2014 by Mary Annslee Urban

All rights reserved. Except for use in any review, the reproduction
or utilization of this work in whole or in part in any form by any
electronic, mechanical or other means, now known or hereinafter
invented, including xerography, photocopying and recording, or in
any information storage or retrieval system, is forbidden without
the written permission of the editorial office, Love Inspired Books,
233 Broadway, New York, NY 10279 U.S.A.

This is a work of fiction. Names, characters, places and incidents are
either the product of the author's imagination or are used fictitiously, and
any resemblance to actual persons, living or dead, business establishments,
events or locales is entirely coincidental.

This edition published by arrangement with Love Inspired Books.

® and TM are trademarks of Love Inspired Books, used under license.
Trademarks indicated with ® are registered in the United States Patent
and Trademark Office, the Canadian Intellectual Property Office and in
other countries.

www.Harlequin.com

Printed in U.S.A.

Let us then with confidence draw near to the throne of grace, that we may receive mercy and find grace to help in time of need.

—*Hebrews* 4:16

This book is affectionately dedicated to the memory of my father, Kenneth Lee Woods, a man whose love for reading and the Lord greatly shaped my life.

Also, to my mother and stepfather, Dee and Bob Gagnon. Your love for family and each other continues to inspire and bless me.

And to my grandchildren, Cameron, Isaac, Jayce and Kylie, who keep me young, laughing and ever amazed.

And most of all to the Lord God for making this book possible.

# ONE

Kylie Harper pressed the cell phone to her ear, her heart thumping against her chest. Had she heard the man right?

Standing outside the airport terminal, she took a moment to gather her composure. Angry clouds hovered low over Asheville, quickly turning the evening into night.

She took a much-needed breath. "Who is this?"

"Murderer." He spoke slowly this time. More precisely. "Because of you, an innocent person died."

Kylie stiffened and swallowed. A sick joke. *Crazed folks enjoy taunting journalists,* her rational self reminded her. "I don't know who you are, what you want or even if you have the right number—"

"Ten years ago." The slow, mumbled drawl bled through the phone line. "I was there."

Clutching the cell in a death grip, Kylie smashed it harder to her ear. Her battered heart dropped to the pit of her stomach. "What do you want?" She tried to sound calm.

A raspy chuckle tore at her eardrums. "Dear Kylie, you do remember what happened ten years ago?"

Silence as her heart now ceased to beat. She pulled the phone from her ear, checked the display. *Restricted number* glared back.

She pressed the phone to her other ear. "Is this about Camp Golden Rock?" The words stuck in her throat.

A bark of laughter replaced the chuckle. "How many incidents are hidden in your past, Kylie? Could I be talking about anything else?"

Kylie gasped, breath caught in her throat.

"I know I've been negligent," the man continued, "not staying in touch. But for this anniversary I planned something special."

Struggling to even breathe, Kylie blocked the memories from her thoughts. So many times she'd relived that May night, haunted by the what-ifs and if-onlys. By God's grace, she'd finally moved on. Put that nightmare behind her.

"Why are you doing this?" she ground out.

"You know how important memories are. Especially the ones that involve death."

*Memories. Anniversaries.* Her ten-year class reunion was coming up. As cruel as it seemed, only one explanation made sense: this had to be a prank. A hidden cameraman from some shock-reality show had to be hiding somewhere. Kylie jerked her gaze around the area.

"You won't find me, Kylie."

She froze. She was being watched.

"The baggage claim, Kylie. My gift is there.

And remember, sweet girl, I'll never be more than a heartbeat away," the man calmly whispered. The phone went dead.

Panic jolted every nerve ending in Kylie's body. Turning on her heel, she rushed back into the terminal and started down the concourse, praying this was a bad joke, but somehow knowing it wasn't.

Leaving caution behind, she bounded down the escalator two steps at a time, her bulky purse banging against her side. On the bottom level and out of breath, she dashed around the corner and into the main baggage claim. She quickly scanned the area. Empty except for the two rental-car agents chatting behind a counter at the opposite end of the building.

She shifted her attention to the flight-status monitor on the wall. Her nerves settled a bit. The last plane for the evening had landed, but the carousel number had yet to be listed. She breathed easier. Nothing. *Thank You, Lord.*

She'd seen this before. Some lonely person fascinated with unsolved murders and too much time on their hands. Why not rouse speculation and gain a little notoriety at the same time? And who better to harass than someone who'd been at the camp, a journalist no less? She shook her head.

A screech, thud and a chime resounded, then carousel A's conveyor belt churned to life.

Kylie turned just in time to see a limp male figure roll down the chute and onto the moving belt.

*No, dear Lord, not again.*

Instantly, the chill returned. Her extremities turned icy about a second before a curdling cry tore from her throat.

Former Delta Force captain Nick Bentley barely roused as the aircraft's front wheels made contact with the runway. The plane bounced, rose in the air and touched down hard again. The final jolt of the impact sent ripples along his spine.

Nick's eyes flew open. He gripped the metal armrests.

Lights flickered on overhead. The thunder of the outside engines assailed his ears.

As he stiffened against the seat back, Nick's adrenaline surged, his mind stumbling to keep up. *What mission are we on? What destination?*

"Welcome to Asheville. The local time is seven thirty-eight," crackled through the commuter's speakers.

*North Carolina.* Nick exhaled heavily as relief swept over him. The nightmare was over.

No more watching over his shoulder.

No more blistering desert heat.

No more death.

*Or?* Tension grabbed at his gut. Was another nightmare about to begin? He was coming home— something he'd vowed he'd never do.

He glanced out the oval window to his left. Runway lights lent an eerie glow against the passing landscape. An outline of rugged mountains. The evergreen beauty was lost in the darkness and fog, but he could picture it still. Lofty hardwoods and bristly pines. Dense forest he used to love.

The plane rolled to a stop. He hung back, waiting for the few other passengers to deplane, then hefted his army-issued duffel bag onto his shoulder and stepped down the steep aircraft stairs and onto the tarmac. The terminal in front of him was lit brightly, surprisingly welcoming. Small and quaint. No bustling crowds to contend with.

Nothing had changed. That was what he was afraid of.

Three back-to-back tours of Afghanistan and Iraq should have prepared him for anything. So why was his gut twisted in knots?

*Temporary assignment,* he reminded himself. Once his brother was back on his feet, he'd shake the dust off his shoes and move on. Find someplace to call home.

He repositioned his duffel and headed for the terminal doors. He inhaled deeply, pulling in a lungful of Blue Ridge air. Cool and clean, yet tainted with memories.

On the ground floor of the main terminal, Kylie stepped aside, allowing a wave of airport security officers a clear path to the baggage-claim conveyor belt and the body sprawled across it.

Two of the officers halted about a yard from the victim and exchanged glances. The older man, shorter and robust, shook his head. His grave expression said it all. The other officer, tall and lanky, craned his neck a bit for a better look but didn't move any closer.

Nausea spiraled through Kylie's abdomen. She struggled to breathe as flashes of another crime erupted in her mind. One just as gruesome. The night her classmate and friend Conrad Miller was killed.

"Late twenties, early thirties is my guess," the tallest officer mumbled after a moment. "Anyone know who he is?" He glanced back at Kylie.

She shook her head. "Not that I can tell."

Approaching sirens blazed to life behind her. The few onlookers, stragglers from earlier flights, were quickly herded out of the way as paramedics and sheriff's deputies rushed in.

There was a cacophony of noise. Questions flying, voices escalating around her. The medics gave a quick assessment of the limp male figure lying in a pool of blood, then pulled a sheet from the gurney and covered him. No other measures were needed.

Kylie backed farther away from the scene and leaned against a nearby column. Coolness from the metal trim penetrated her thin jacket, adding to her chill. Fortunately, she'd gathered sufficient facts for a story, along with an elusive phone call. Nothing conclusive, but enough to satisfy her boss, chief news editor Max Dawson. And after a cliff-hanger article for the morning paper, she planned to hand the story over to another colleague. Being at the wrong place at the right time—even worse, being the perpetrator's contact person—didn't make her the best fit for the story. Hopefully, Max would agree.

"Kylie, tell me again what you know." Detective Dave Michelson walked toward her, scratching his forehead with the end of his pen.

"I really don't know much." Kylie straightened a bit, willing her knees not to buckle. "I came to the airport to drop off my sister and was heading back to my car when I received the phone call."

"And the man on the phone told you he had a gift for you at baggage claim?"

"Eventually. Yes."

"Any idea who the caller might be?" Dave started scribbling on a pad.

"No. He spoke with a thick, muffled drawl. And the number came up restricted."

"Was there anyone else around when the body arrived?"

"Security was right behind me. Tipped off by

a caller...or killer." Just saying the word sent a shiver dancing across her skin.

Dave grunted, shifted his husky frame and kept writing.

"The first security guard at the scene checked for a wallet or ID," Kylie added, tightening her arms across her chest. "None were found."

Dave bobbed his head. "No signs of life?"

Her heart fractured. "None. He was bleeding from the neck."

Eyebrows gathered over Dave's prominent nose. He didn't comment, only jotted more notes on his pad.

"Fortunately, security officers secured everything before a crowd formed. Not really a picture that bystanders needed to see." She knew that from experience.

A grunt again. Dave hadn't changed since high school. Serial grunts, nods, maybe a raised eyebrow. He only said what he needed to.

"Thanks." He pocketed his pen and pad.

This time she nodded. There was nothing else to say.

"Incoming bags are on carousel C," one of the security guards shouted, gesturing to the opposite side of the baggage-claim area for the passengers stepping off the escalator. "Just keep moving."

There were surprised looks and mumbles from the travelers, but everyone complied, except for one man. He was dressed in fatigues and boots, a duffel draped over his shoulder and a canned drink in his hand. His dark, piercing gaze roved over the scene. And as he stood there, his expression turned dismal.

Kylie's teeth dug into her bottom lip. She knew that expression. And she would never forget those eyes.

Nick Bentley.

Nick stared at the scene and nearly lost the burger he'd just devoured. The thread of welcome he'd felt when he arrived evaporated. A déjà vu moment replaced it.

EMS workers strapped the body wrapped in a bloodstained sheet onto the gurney and headed out the door. Three police officers followed and several others remained at the crime scene, talking among themselves and shaking their heads. As they had the night Conrad Miller was murdered.

Ten years ago, Nick's senior class had taken a trip to nearby Camp Golden Rock. Their last night there, somewhere between eight and nine o'clock, Conrad's body had been dumped onto the front porch of their cabin. He had been found lying in a small pool of blood, with his throat slashed from ear to ear. Nick swallowed as nausea threatened again. Conrad had taken security patrol that night. It was his job to make sure everyone was out of their cabin and at the bonfire. A mandatory buddy system was in place, but Conrad's buddy had been late.

Nick still couldn't forgive himself.

"Nick."

A wave of panicked voices echoed around him, but the softness of one feminine tone cut through the mayhem, making him almost drop his duffel and the drink that he was carrying. Nick hadn't been home an hour and already his mind was playing tricks on him. He slowly turned his head and to his surprise, he met Kylie Harper's warm green gaze. Shoulder-length auburn curls framed her sweet face. Pert nose, slender brows, high cheekbones, luscious full lips. An unmistakable twinge of awareness shot through him, quicker than any bullets he'd dodged in the Middle East.

He blinked, not believing how even after ten years she still struck him as the most beautiful girl he'd ever seen. His déjà vu moment got stronger.

"Kylie." Even saying her name stung. Another part of his life he'd tried to forget.

"I can't believe it's you." She stared up at him and brushed stray locks back with her fingers.

No ring. He couldn't help but notice.

"Yeah. It's been a while." He swung his duffel to the ground, propping his drink can on top. "And a dead body wasn't exactly the welcome I hoped for."

"Ironic, isn't it?" Shaking her head, she looked up at him, her eyes widening and brimming with tears. "The poor man. No one even knows who he is. Even worse—"

She looked away a moment, took a deep breath.

"Worse?" Nick stuffed his hands into his jacket packets.

Another moment, then her gaze settled back on him, fear in her eyes. "I think Conrad's killer may be back." Her voice was barely a whisper.

The knife in Nick's heart slipped a little deeper. "What do you mean, *back?* You don't think—"

Kylie's nod cut off his words. Déjà vu had just escalated to nightmare.

# TWO

At Milkweed Café in downtown Asheville, Kylie gazed at Nick from across the table. He was tall and lean, with a Go Army black T-shirt stretched across his wide shoulders and chest. He looked so mature. Strong features, chiseled just right, and his eyes a deep brown as rich as the cola he was drinking.

As handsome as she dared to remember.

This Delta Force captain left no one in doubt of his capabilities.

A warm comfort swept over her. She still felt safe in his presence.

Nick took a drink and set the glass on the table. "Do you really think this murder is related to Conrad's?" His deltoid muscles bulged slightly as he eased back into his seat.

Biting the inside of her lip, Kylie shrugged. "That's the question I keep asking myself. The man on the phone said that he was there the night Conrad died. Although it seems odd—silence for ten years and then…this."

"Could be a copycat." Nick crossed his arms against his sturdy chest. "If so, this butcher has done his research and probably knows as much about the crime as we do. Or more."

"That's true. I just wish he hadn't involved me."

Nick chuckled. "Journalists do attract flakes."

"Flakes I can handle." She nodded. "But murderers—"

"You know—" Nick cut her off, sat forward and looked at her, suspicion skewing his features. "In all likelihood, you know this guy."

Her spine prickled. "What?"

"The murderer. He knew your cell number and that you'd be at the airport. Even knew what time."

Kylie shivered. The very thought made her skin crawl. "I hadn't even considered that."

Nick's dark brows drew closer. "Who knew you'd be at the airport tonight?"

Leaning on her elbows, she mentally ticked off everyone who might have known her plans to drop off her sister. Her chest tightened at the results. "There's too many to name. I left work early, so most of my colleagues were aware. Shannon and I went to a church social last night. Lots of people asked when she and the baby were leaving."

"You never could hide much in this small town." Nick nodded. "Except possibly murder."

A boulder-size knot formed in Kylie's stomach. "I can't imagine anyone I know being capable of such a terrible crime. Not now or ten years ago." She dropped her voice several octaves.

Nick touched her arm, sending shivers of a different manner across her skin. "Kylie, predators aren't obvious. Believe me, I've met my share. Sometimes it's who you'd least expect."

The strained expression in Kylie's eyes ignited a deep burn in Nick's chest. Breathing deep, the scent of her perfume filtered into his nostrils. Something sweet and subtle. A hundred percent intriguing.

A hundred percent Kylie.

His heart gave a solid kick against his ribs. A few minutes with this woman and already he'd ventured onto dangerous ground. He broke eye contact with her and forced his mixed-up emotions to quiet.

Their dreams of a life together had blown apart with the tragedy at Camp Golden Rock. After that, Nick could barely live with himself, let alone offer anything to Kylie. He'd needed to get away from Asheville, start fresh with nothing to hold him back.

He swirled the liquid in his glass, the ice clinking. An impulsive decision.

But a mistake? He'd never know that for sure.

Now that he was back, one look into Kylie's eyes and long-buried emotions sparked to life. A jolt of remembered love, but also a tug in his chest that reminded him that those days were over.

The past was behind them. They were older now. Wiser. They had both moved on in very different directions.

The waitress walked by. He held up his hand to catch her attention. "May I get a refill, please?"

The woman nodded and he glanced at Kylie. "Would you like anything? You barely touched your coffee."

Kylie shook her head. "No, thank you. I'm fine."

Though concern shadowed her eyes, her voice came across confident.

Nick's gut clenched. Seeing her unsettled and worried, his protective instincts surged. The events at the airport had been horrific enough. He shouldn't have voiced his opinions so quickly. He mentally kicked himself for adding more distress to her day.

The need to comfort her rose. "Don't rack your brain trying to figure this guy out. He may not be anyone you know. Right now, facts don't support any theory." He covered his own concerns with a grin.

A glint of relief entered her eyes. She nodded. "Thanks, that makes me feel better."

Good. Now if only he could convince himself.

Quiet fell between them. And then Kylie settled back in her chair. "Enough talk about murder. I'd like to give my brain a break, at least until I get home. I have an article due by four."

He glanced at his watch. Nearly ten o'clock. "Do you need to leave and get started?"

She raked her hand through her long hair, tousling her curls further. "No, I'm fine."

"Well, then, tell me how you've been." He asked the question that had crossed his mind often over the past ten years.

"Me?"

"Yes, you." Nick nodded and folded his arms, enjoying the view a little too much. Although appreciating a woman's beauty wasn't a crime. Even if she was his ex-girlfriend.

Kylie fell silent and picked up her cup and drank deeply from it.

Nick reclined against the seat back, his gaze resting on her as he waited. She must have quite a story to tell. He might be sorry he asked.

After a moment, Kylie set down her cup with a clink. Ever since high school, her life had gone by in a blur—at least in the romance department, as her parents so readily liked to point out. As if having a husband would solve the world's problems or create a life of happily ever after. That fairy tale had died a long time ago. Thanks to Nick Bentley.

A sigh crawled up her throat. She swallowed it back. No telling how many relationships Nick had been involved in since they'd split up.

Not that it should matter. She picked up a napkin and dabbed the sides of her mouth. He no longer had any effect on her. She met his eyes, the tenderness in his dark gaze unmistakable. A tingle rippled along her spine.

Okay, maybe a little.

"I'm waiting." Nick's gaze sharpened on her face, which she feared was now blushing crimson.

She cleared her throat and spoke. "Well, I attended college at UNC Asheville and graduated with a degree in journalism. And, as you know, I work at the *Asheville Daily News*." She folded her hands on the table. "What about you?"

A deep chuckle rumbled from his chest. "Hey, not so fast."

She blinked and then swallowed. "That's about it. Really."

He arched a dark brow. "No wedding bells or kids?"

She shook her head no.

This time both eyebrows lifted. "No special someone in your life?"

*Not anymore.* "Nope."

His smoldering gaze warmed her deep inside. Nick hadn't changed. He never settled for elusive. Always wanted the whole story and never gave in until he got it—well, except after Conrad's murder. Her heart squeezed. After that he'd seemed to lose interest in everything. Including her. She took another drink of coffee, bitter against her suddenly dry throat.

Nick ran his hands over his close-cropped hair. "Wow, I thought you'd be married by now. A house. A couple kids."

At one time she would have expected the same.

"I'm only twenty-eight. Not quite an old maid. Although my parents might disagree."

Nick laughed fully this time, a rumble as deep as a chasm, and charming dimples dented his cheeks. Her heart skipped a beat. "No, I wouldn't put you in the old-maid category yet. By the way, how are your parents?"

"Enjoying retirement in Florida. My sister and her family joined them last year."

"And you? Any plans to go?"

"No. Asheville is home. I love it here."

"That's what I thought." He grimaced.

An awful coldness seeped through her, filtering out into her extremities. Nick was still running from the past. Ten long years hadn't changed that.

Breathing deep, Kylie strove not to let her emotions show. She leaned forward, propped her elbow on the edge of the table and rested her chin in her hand. "Now, tell me about you."

"Well." He shrugged. "I'm in town to help out with the family hardware store until Steven is back on his feet. He took it over a few years back when my parents retired and moved to Charlotte to care for my grandfather."

"That's right. I heard Steven had been in an accident."

"Yep. Fell off a bicycle. He rode off a trail trying to impress some new girlfriend with his agile riding skills. Tumbled about twenty feet before briar bushes cushioned his fall."

Kylie winced. "Not much of a cushion."

Nick shook his head. "No, not hardly. He broke his left femur and ankle, dislocated his shoulder, and worst of all, the girlfriend ditched him."

"So sorry."

"Kind of ironic." He chuckled. "I've dodged bullets in the heaviest war zones in the world and he almost kills himself falling off a bike."

"I'm sure you're not going to let him forget that."

Another chuckle. "No way."

She hated to ask, but she did. "Any special someone in your life?"

When Nick paused, her heart gave an irrational thump. Her rotten day took another nosedive. Kylie picked up her drink and took a sip, feigning nonchalance. She wanted to be apathetic about Nick, distanced from the pain of a teenager's broken heart. Whatever infatuation they'd shared had died along with Conrad. It was time to grow up and move—

"No one special," he finally blurted.

Her heart danced in her chest. She looked up and caught him staring at her. His firm mouth twitched into a smile, deepening the glint in his rich dark eyes.

Heat rose up Kylie's neck. She hoped he couldn't read her mind. She managed a stiff smile. "Well, there's still time. You're not over-the-hill yet, either." Crazy to even care.

Silence stretched between them.

She set down her cup and leaned a fraction closer, ready to change the conversation to something less personal. "Tell me about the army."

"The army." Nick smiled slightly. Settling back in his seat, he linked his hands behind his head. "Let's see. I served ten years. During that time, I witnessed too much war, too much destruction and too much death."

Images of recent news-broadcast footage assembled in Kylie's mind. Her heartbeat stumbled. She couldn't believe Nick had been in the middle of that. "Delta Forces, I hear. Pretty intense?"

He nodded his head. "Could be. Even brutal at times. But good came out of it. Lives were saved."

Admiration for his commitment filled her chest. "Will you be going back?"

"Nope. I've done my time."

Kylie smiled; she couldn't help it. "Well, you're quite the hero around here."

"Hero." Nick straightened in his chair. His jovial expression turned stormy. "Hero is the last thing I'll ever be around here."

"The story is yours, Kylie." Max shifted his stance and pulled open the file drawer.

"But Doug Landers is ready to jump in." Kylie fought off a sigh. "At the moment, I can't even differentiate between facts and emotions."

Max pulled several folders from the cabinet and shut the drawer with a clink. "Use it to your advantage. Make the story real. Passion, pain, every emotion will bleed through the pages and grip the readers."

*Great.* Kylie exhaled, blowing out slowly. "Reporters are supposed to be objective, Max, not part of the story. I'll be happy to consult, edit Doug's draft and even give an interview."

"It's yours, Kylie." Max tossed the files on his desk. "Keep it real. Keep it fresh. Keep it coming. Hopefully, the madman will call again."

"Uh, thanks. But once was plenty."

"By the way, I contacted the Asheville police this morning. They've got some newsworthy facts waiting for you."

"Wonderful." Kylie turned and plodded out the door, praying for patience and a speedy resolution to this murder.

She headed outside and into the bright afternoon sunshine. Max was even crazier than usual. Hoping the killer would call again. She shivered at the thought.

Kylie was still wrestling with annoyance when she parked in front of the municipal building. She pulled her notepad from her satchel and got out of the car. Taking a deep breath, she hiked up her chin and squared her shoulders. *Okay.* She could do this. She segued into reporter mode, forcing her attention from all discomforting thoughts. If she had to do this assignment, she'd give it her best.

She hiked her purse higher on her shoulder and walked into the building.

In the main lobby, she checked in with the clerk and wound her way down the first-floor hall, which teemed with attorneys and their clients, catching snatches of agitated conversation on her way to the elevator. She stepped in and punched the button to the fourth floor. The elevator started to rise, lurched, then ground to a halt. The lights blinked off.

Blackness filled Kylie's view. *Okay.* She ordered herself to stay calm. She dug into her purse and captured her phone. With the touch of her finger the cell fired up. She used it as a light to locate the panel of buttons on the wall. She punched four. Nothing. Then she flipped the emergency switch. Same.

Drumming her fingers against the side of her thigh, she waited. Auxiliary power should kick on any moment. Several long moments passed.

She punched the floor button again. Gears screeched, the car rattled, no other movement.

If maintenance was affected by the recent city budget cuts, she was quickly becoming a proponent for higher taxes.

Kylie inhaled, the air already stuffy. She fumbled to punch 911 on her phone and held it to her ear. Silence. *No service.*

With all the people in the building, maintenance had to have been notified by now. Reasonable thoughts, which rapidly deteriorated with each passing second.

"Anytime now." She spoke to the emptiness around her.

Lights blinked on.

"Thank you." She drew in a breath of relief.

The elevator edged up one floor before slamming to a halt, knocking Kylie off-balance. With arms flailing, she reached for the handrail to steady herself, but the car lurched again, the force so great that her feet went out from under her. She went down hard, her bare knees smashing into the floor. Darkness blinded her again.

*Lord, I'm getting nervous here.* Kylie picked herself up. Clenching the handrail with one hand, she used the other to smooth her skirt.

Pain searing through her, she grabbed for a calming breath.

Music trickled into the car and broke the silence. Eerie and empty as the air around her.

Her heartbeat picked up. For a breathless second, the horror of the previous night suffocated all logic. *Never more than a heartbeat away...*

The caller's words ripped through her mind. Panic bottled in her chest, making it hard to breathe. Was he close by? Could he be watching her?

*Calm down.* She forced her breathing to slow. She'd watched too many old episodes of *The Twilight Zone* with her sister.

A jolt, then emergency lights flickered on, casting a dull glow around her. The elevator started to rise, steadily ascending, passing the third floor, then the fourth. Kylie stared at the glowing numbers, willing the car to stop. It didn't matter where, she was getting off.

Halfway between the fifth and sixth floors, the elevator stalled.

Patience evaporated, Kylie slammed her fingers into the buttons on the panel. The elevator inched upward.

*Please, Lord, help me get out of here.*

She pressed her back into the corner of the car, bracing herself and whispering prayers as her fingers white-knuckled the wooden handrail. She held her breath. A second passed. A pulley squealed. The elevator made a rapid descent, whizzing down the shaft. She closed her eyes, teeth gritted, her pulse thumping steadily in her ears.

Just when she thought all hope was gone, the car stopped and bounced. A scream caught in her throat, shock and fear rising as she lurched forward.

For a frozen moment, Kylie regained her breath and flipped the emergency switch again. Lights flashed for a half second before darkness shrouded her.

"Help!" She startled at the shrill echo of her voice.

*Stay calm.* Short breaths billowed from her lungs.

One moment. Two—not working. "Help me!" She pounded on the wall. "Somebody get me out of here!"

Lights flickered on. The elevator started to ascend. She slumped against the wall again and watched as the blinking numbers above the door rose. Two. Three. Four. The lumbering machine finally ground to a jittery stop. As the heavy doors screeched open, she burst out and collided with a broad uniformed chest.

After a stunned moment, Kylie grasped the situation. She inched back and lifted her gaze. A pair of amused blue eyes stared back at her.

"Hello, Kylie. Are you okay?"

"The elevator." She gestured behind her before slapping a trembling hand against her rapidly beating chest. "I was trapped. No lights. The elevator stalled, then fell—" She ran out of breath before finishing.

A wrinkle formed between Detective Dave Michelson's eyes. "Security called about someone stuck between floors. You must have been the one screaming."

Several other officers stood around him. With shrugs and mumbles, the group dispersed.

Half embarrassed, half relieved, Kylie nodded, and a breath flitted between her teeth.

"I've never been trapped in an elevator before," she mumbled, for a lack of anything better to say.

"It happens sometimes." Dave scratched beside

his nose. "Probably just an electrical malfunction. The maintenance crew is already looking into it."

*Just a malfunction?* She forced a nod, her heart still racing.

The day was not shaping up as she'd hoped.

# THREE

Inside the municipal building, Nick trekked up the last flight of stairs and stepped onto the fourth floor. As he wandered down the hall toward the police department, the sound of a woman's anxious tone quickened his steps.

A few weeks ago, he'd left the military and vowed to leave his training behind, live a peaceful life and mind his own business.

Too late. His heart rate sped up and his thoughts churned into full investigative mode.

He rounded the corner, his rapid steps heavy against the wood floor as he entered the elevator lobby. To his surprise, Kylie stood in plain view in front of the elevator. Her glossy dark hair, tied in a ponytail, bounced against her slender neck as she pivoted to look at him.

"Nick."

He wagged his brows. "We have to stop meeting like this."

An uncertain smile quivered up at him. An unexpected heat filled his chest. She was getting to him, all right.

"Nick Bentley," the tall, burly officer greeted him, redirecting his thoughts.

Nick shook Dave's outstretched hand. "It's been a while, Dave. Hope you're doing well."

"Just fine." Dave canted his head toward Kylie. "I wish I could say the same for her."

Nick met Kylie's concerned gaze. "Still a little unnerved about last night?"

She half nodded and then shrugged. "You could say that. Add a heart-racing ride in a possessed elevator and, well…my nerves haven't settled quite yet."

"So you were the one stuck in the elevator?"

She bobbed her head, looking dismayed. "Yes, I was. And I wouldn't recommend a ride like that to anyone."

He gave a slight chuckle. "Are you okay?"

She pushed hair from her face. "A little frazzled, but fine."

"I can understand you being on edge after last night's events. I've had a tough time getting the murder off my mind. I came by this morning in hopes of gathering a few details. Apparently you did also."

"Yes. Sorry to say."

"Another article?"

Kylie answered his question with a tight smile.

Curiosity brightened Dave's expression. "Nick, you're in law enforcement, aren't you? Part of the military police?"

"Something like that."

"Delta Force. The army's most elite top secret task force," Kylie put in.

Nick still couldn't believe Kylie had kept up with him. A wave of guilt tightened his chest. To think how hard he had worked to forget this town…and her.

Dave nodded. "You sound like a good resource to have around here. Small town or not, the department stays busy, but mostly due to being understaffed. I'm chief investigator, with only three on my staff. If you have time, any input would be appreciated. We're not too well versed on murders of this caliber."

"I don't know about that." Nick waved off the compliment. "I'm sure you guys are more than capable, but I'll be happy to take a look at any evidence you have."

Dave ushered them into a corner office under the speculative gazes of other law-enforcement personnel.

Nick took a seat beside Kylie. Dave shut the glass door and joined them at the table.

"So, what do you know so far about our John Doe?" Kylie started, flipping open her notepad.

Dave folded his thick fingers on the marred wooden table. "The forensics team is working on the details. What we do know is that robbery wasn't the motive. The victim's wallet was discovered in some bushes a block from the homeless shelter on Oakmont. There were eighty-eight dollars in it, along with his ID and Social Security card."

Nick figured as much. "So who was this unlucky person?"

Dave adjusted his bulky frame in his seat and canted his head. "The victim was Robert Tucker. He lived at the shelter. Showed up here about a month ago. No one there knows much about him. He pretty much kept to himself."

"Anyone see him the day of the murder?" Nick sorted through some pictures of the victim on the table.

"Actually, earlier in the day Tucker was in an altercation with another patron of the shelter and he was asked to leave."

Kylie stopped writing and glanced up from her notes. "Do you consider the man Tucker had the altercation with a suspect?"

Dave gave a firm shake of his head. "No, we've already ruled him out. He ended up in the hospital with a broken arm and head fracture and is still there."

"Nice guy, Tucker was." Nick gave a low whistle.

"Did Tucker have any issues with anyone else at the shelter?" Kylie scratched her temple with the end of her pen.

Dave shrugged. "At the moment we don't have those details."

A lump formed in Nick's throat. His hope for a quick resolution to this case slipped away. "Do you have any suspects at the moment?"

"No. That's something we're working on." A flat coolness blanketed Dave's tone.

If Nick hadn't known Dave, he would have thought years on the force had made him callous. A coping strategy Nick had seen often. Hardened to the tragedies of others. One of the reasons he'd left.

"Does anyone at the shelter have information on Tucker's family members, distant or local?" Kylie's hopeful tone escalated a bit.

A shrug from Dave. "Not that I'm aware."

Kylie noted a couple more details on her pad.

Nick's mind raced with questions. But only one seemed pertinent. "The victim was bleeding from a wound on the neck, correct?"

When Dave nodded, Kylie finished his question. "Is that what he died from?"

"Seems to be. His throat was slit and he bled through his carotid artery."

Several seconds passed. Nick waited for Dave to elaborate further. When he didn't, Nick had to ask. "Slit from ear to ear?"

A hesitation, then Dave nodded.

Kylie stopped writing. Her gaze snagged Nick's and her face paled. "Exactly like Conrad."

"Afraid so." Dave's voice went low. "We're already looking into a possible link to Conrad's unsolved murder."

Nick's heart dropped like a piece of lead to his stomach.

That was what he was afraid of.

"He's back. I know he is." Kylie's rapid pace didn't slow as she headed for her car. "Why would he come back after all these years? And why would he contact me?"

"Nothing's conclusive yet. He still could be a copycat looking for press. Everything about Conrad's murder is public knowledge." Nick lengthened his stride to keep up with her.

At the car, Kylie halted and blinked up at him. "Slit throat, yes. But from ear to ear... Only a few of us knew about that."

"Kylie, word travels. But even if this was Conrad's killer, he may not strike again for another ten years."

She threw up her hands. "Or maybe he's already picked his next victim?"

Even as Nick tried to console her, to relieve her concerns, the same questions plagued him.

"Just be careful. Okay?"

Kylie narrowed her eyes on him. "So you do think I'm in danger."

Nick held up his hand. "Kylie, I didn't say that. Although it's never a bad idea to play it safe."

She swung hair back from her face and huffed softly. "This whole situation creeps me out."

"It should."

She gave a small laugh. "At least my reaction is appropriate."

He smiled. That was the Kylie he remembered. Always a trouper. "By the way, do you have a security system at home?"

She brushed a soft brown curl behind her ear with an uneasy gesture. "Not yet. I recently moved into my grandmother's old house."

He nodded, recalling the small timber-frame home, nestled in the trees and bordered by national forest. "She had a great view of the Smokies, I recall."

"Still does. As beautiful as ever. Although rural and isolated. My closest neighbors are two acres away."

"Yeah. I remember that, too."

Nick's conscience would never let him forget how he'd once turned his back on Kylie and walked away. He'd already let her down once when she needed him. And if anything happened to her now...well, he hated to fathom that. "I don't think it's a bad idea to err on the side of caution and stay somewhere else for a few days, let things blow over. My brother has an extra room at his house. I'm bunking next door in the apartment above the store."

She rubbed at the wrinkle that formed between

her brows. "Thanks for the offer, Nick. I'm going to try to keep things in perspective, like you said. Besides, Dave had that tracer put on my phone line. If the creep calls again, hopefully, they'll track him down in short order."

Optimistic, but not realistic. Nick breathed deep. "Keeping things in perspective doesn't mean you can't take precautions."

"If things get more harried, I'll consider your offer. How is Steven, anyway?"

"Still in the hospital and going through rehab."

Kylie curved her lips in a sympathetic smile that any starlet would envy. Lovely curved lips, luscious and full, eminently kissable... Nick blinked. He squared his shoulders and lifted his chin. He wasn't going there. Once his brother was ready to get back to work again, he'd be on his way. He had no intention of hanging around.

"Speaking of Steven." Nick cleared his throat. "I should check in on him and get back to the store."

Her brow creased. For an instant she just stared at him, and then her face relaxed a bit. "Sorry you had to get involved in this mess. But I do appreciate your help and concern."

Before he had the chance to tell her he was glad to be of assistance, Kylie turned away, pulling open the car door and slipping behind the wheel.

"Say hello to Steven for me," she called out her open window as she revved up the engine and backed out of the parking spot.

"Be careful and don't forget about the room offer," he called after her, his words trailing, carried away by the breeze.

Tension strummed through every muscle, reminding him to keep a close eye on Kylie.

There was little traffic, so the ride to the hospital took only a few minutes. The woman at the information desk directed Nick to the first set of elevators and told him to get off on the third floor, the rehab unit.

The door to Steven's room stood ajar. Nick inched it farther open and heard chuckles from the other side of the pulled curtain. Stepping farther into the room, he cleared his throat. A tall blonde dressed in green scrubs yanked the fabric drapery back.

Steven sat in a reclining chair in the corner of the room, his casted leg elevated and his arm in a sling resting on a pillow. His face lit up. "Bro, welcome."

Nick stepped closer. "I hope I'm not interrupting anything."

"No, no." Steven waved his good arm toward the woman in scrubs. "This is my physical therapist, Amy. We just had a therapy session and she was helping me get comfortable."

Nick nodded. "I see."

"Well, Steven, I'll check back with you later." Amy brushed past Nick and slipped out the door.

"See you later, Amy," Steven called after her. His gaze bounced to Nick. "I was expecting you sooner. I thought you got into town last night."

"I did. But by the time I got to your place it was too late to call or come by." Nick moved closer to his brother and extended his hand. "I'd give you a hug, but I'm afraid I don't have Amy's gentle touch."

"No problem." Steven laughed as he shook Nick's hand. "Good to see you. I hate that your plane got in late. I know you had a long trip."

"Actually, we landed on time. I just ran into an old friend."

"Nice." Steven chuckled. "I'm laid up in bed and you ditched me for an old friend."

"I wouldn't say I ditched you, although it looks like you've been in good hands." Nick lifted a brow.

"Oh, yeah. What can I say? Women love me." The pleasant smirk on Steven's face made Nick laugh.

"So who was this old friend you ran into?" Steven winced as he adjusted his sling.

Nick pulled a chair to the side of Steven's recliner, angling it toward him. "Kylie Harper."

"Kylie?" Steven eyes rounded. "I would think she's more than an old friend."

She had been once, but those days were gone. And at the moment, Nick had no intention of rehashing those memories. "Have you seen the news today?"

With his brow knitted, Steven said, "No, why?"

"There was a murder at the airport last night. I ran into Kylie in the baggage claim as the body was being removed from the scene."

"Wow. Pretty creepy. Was Kylie there covering the story?"

Nick shook his head. "No. She was contacted by the killer and he directed her to the victim. An unknown man with his throat slit."

"What?" Steven sat upright in his chair before slumping against the back again. "Ow!"

Nick jumped up from his chair. "What can I do?"

"Adjust my leg a little to the left and place the pillow back under my sling."

Nick did as his brother asked.

"Throat slit?" Steven said through gritted teeth. "Coincidence, or is Conrad's killer back?"

"That's what I'm hoping to find out."

Steven blew out a slow breath, the pain erasing from his face. "Are you helping with the investigation?"

"Dave Michelson is the detective on the case and I've offered my services."

A small smile crept across Steven's face. "Good. Then this killer is toast."

"Well, it's a little early to predict that, but let's hope so."

"Hope so? I know so. With your passion for justice, this guy doesn't have a chance."

Nick swallowed. He knew better than anyone that sometimes that wasn't enough.

# FOUR

Max had planted himself in the chair to the right of Kylie's desk and it looked as though it would take a three-alarm fire to roust him out. If not for the tedious click of the chair as he rocked back and forth, his presence would have been easier to ignore.

"Big news in a small-town paper. That's what puts us on the map."

"Uh-huh." Kylie hit the delete key on her computer keyboard again, erasing the last paragraph of her upcoming article. She didn't need another distraction. Between last night's murder, Nick's sudden reappearance and the elevator episode, her mind was already stretched to capacity.

Max continued to ramble, giving his usual pep talk. "If you put your heart and soul into your work, there may be a Pulitzer at the other end..."

She just wanted to make it to the end of the day without melting into a mental pile of mush.

Kylie studied the computer screen. The words blurred together. She needed to get a grip. Focus on what really mattered—writing this article.

Apparently her mind didn't agree. At the moment her thoughts revolved around one thing: Nick Bentley.

A wave of nostalgia wrapped around her. It didn't help that Nick hadn't changed one iota in the past ten years…well…with the exception of bulging muscles and close-cropped hair. Still, his dimpled smile and those warm brown eyes sent her heart into a gallop. This completely defied logic, given his rapid departure after their high-school graduation and that she hadn't had so much as a phone call since.

Their breakup had been amicable to some degree. They'd both had guilt and sadness to deal with after Conrad's death. They'd needed space. But she'd always thought…well, always hoped that one day—

*Stop it.* Kylie shook herself and started pecking on the keyboard again, trying to untangle her thoughts and write the article. She needed to leave history where it belonged—behind her.

Nick was home for one reason. And it wasn't her.

She gave a little sigh that came out more like a moan. Biting her lip, she glanced at Max. He continued to rock and ramble. Tall and wiry, he looked about as uncomfortable in the chair as she was about him sitting there in it. She started typing again.

"Now, if the killer calls again, don't forget your journalistic duties and ask him a few questions."

At the word *killer,* her ears perked up. She spun in her chair and confronted Max. "So if I get another call from this guy, you want me to interview him. Like what? A prize boxer after a fight? Asking him how good it feels to win?"

Max threw his head back and barked with laughter. "Kylie, girl. You've got more wit than I give you credit for."

"No, Max. I'm serious. If this man calls again, the conversation will involve his agenda, not mine."

Max pushed his thick-rimmed glasses up on his nose. "Well, any clue to his whereabouts, motive or even his next victim is what readers want to know."

*Readers?* Kylie fell back in her chair and covered her face with her hands. "You're talking about a murderer, Max. A cold-blooded killer. Not some bad-boy sports figure. Let's pray for a speedy resolution to this murder case and for life to get back to normal."

"Until then, keep the story alive and interesting." Max stood and stretched a little. "Pulitzer, Kylie." He gave her a pat on the shoulder on his way out of the newsroom.

Forget the Pulitzer. She'd be happy with a little quiet and peace of mind.

She skimmed the article, edited a couple sentences and added a few more facts, grateful to see it was coming together. A little more tweaking and she'd be finished.

The trill of her cell phone sent her pulse into a

sprint. She pulled the handset from under a stack of papers. *Restricted* showed on the screen. She pressed it to her ear. "Kylie Harper."

"Kylie. My dear Kylie, how are you?"

Her heart stopped. She shifted the phone to the other ear. "Who are you? What do you want?"

"Don't sound so fussy, dear. Didn't you enjoy my gift?"

Kylie swallowed a gasp. "A dead man? No. That's a terrible gift."

Heated laughter rippled through the line.

She pinched her eyes shut and whispered through clenched teeth, "Please, stop this madness."

"Stop?" Another fiery chuckle. "Why, precious, I've just begun."

Kylie bolted upright in her chair. Her eyes popped open. "What do you mean?"

"Did you enjoy the elevator ride, Kylie?"

Her heart slipped. "You…you were responsible for that?"

"I told you. I'm never far away."

*Questions? Questions?* Max's words echoed in her head. What questions should she ask? She rubbed at her forehead as if to jump-start her brain. "So where are you now?"

"Too personal, dear. But I have a question for you. Fireworks. Do you remember?"

*Fireworks?* "I don't know what you are talking about."

"Oh, but you do."

"No—"

"The cows and the moon."

"What?"

"I saw you stealing kisses, Kylie."

Fighting for a full breath, Kylie barely got out, "Jake Plyler's farm."

"Another gift awaits you there."

*Click.*

After a phone call to the police and another call to update Nick, Kylie tossed her cell phone onto the passenger seat and tightened her grip on the steering wheel of her midsize sedan. On a usual spring day there would be another couple hours of daylight left, but nothing about this day was usual. Dark gray clouds hovered low in the sky, heralding an approaching storm, as dismal and menacing as the anxiety clutching her chest.

She took a breath to ease it, reminding herself that she was just following a story. Doing her job.

This wasn't personal.

She clung to the reassuring thought.

At Adams Gap, Kylie left the parkway and turned down a heavily rutted two-lane dirt road. The Plyler farm had been vacant for the past six years and she hadn't traveled this path in twice that long. Not since the spring festival, her sophomore year of high school.

An impromptu after-party.

It was a clear, breezy night, she recalled, scented by the crackling fire, a bonfire licking the darkness and strains of music resonating from portable speakers. Blankets and homemade quilts peppered the grass field beside the barn and couples snuggled together to watch an amateur fireworks display put on by fellow classmates.

For most of that year, she had admired Nick from afar. A crush nursed along by his contagious laughter and impish grin. She could still remember the tingle of excitement she'd felt when he'd asked her to be his date. And on that clear May night beneath a star-studded sky, they'd shared their first kiss—a moment that hadn't gone unnoticed by many of their razzing friends, and a moment she'd never forget.

Up ahead, an old battered stop sign marked the end of the route. Kylie's car bumped over the uneven road. She made the final turn around a sharp bend. A tingle of relief swept through her when she saw several squad cars already there. Police officers and local deputies swarmed the area, tramping through overgrown weeds and grass. Body-recovering dogs accompanied them.

Goose bumps blazed a trail up her arms.

She swallowed hard, trying to shove back the lump of fear that nearly choked her and failing miserably.

*Lord, help me.*

\* \* \*

The moment Nick answered his cell phone and heard panic in Kylie's voice, he jumped out of his office chair, grabbed his keys and bolted out the back exit of the store. There was danger in the air and she was in the middle of it.

He gunned Steven's motorcycle, his wheels kicking up dirt and gravel, leaving a dusty cloud in his wake. Leaning into the curve, he throttled his bike around the corner and fought against the force of anxiety pressing down on his chest.

His visit to Asheville was supposed to be short, quiet and uneventful.

Not happening.

He slowed his speed as a weather-beaten barn came into view. Jake Plyler's old farm.

It was time to finally put the fears of the past behind him. Reconnect with family and friends. Help track down and maybe even catch a serial killer. Conrad's killer. Sweet restitution.

He tried to hold on to the good thoughts, even as he experienced the niggling urge to turn his bike around and hightail it back to the airport. Get out of Asheville and never return.

A temptation he wouldn't give in to. For Kylie's sake.

Nick pulled to the edge of the pasture and parked his bike. Several short pieces of rusty, twisted wire projected from a corner post, marking where the fence had once been. He shed his leather gloves and hung his helmet from one of the handlebars. For a long moment he stood there and assessed the scene. In every direction, officers scoured the grounds, flashlights beaming. A helicopter circled above, blazing a path of white light across the dusky sky, and newscasters reported live in front of video-slinging cameramen.

*Chaos* was the first thought that came to Nick's mind.

*Kylie* was the second.

He took off down the gravel drive toward the barn. She was his main concern. His only concern. He was grateful she'd called to keep him in the loop.

"Nick."

He stopped short as a male voice called his name.

The side door of the barn slammed against the craggy wood siding as Dave Michelson walked out. "You're just in time."

"What do you know, Dave?" Nick turned and headed toward him.

"Not much. In fact, we're batting zero." Dave put both hands on his hips and a pucker of frustration furrowed his forehead.

"Nothing?" Nick took another look around. The grounds rambled on for acres. Overgrown fields melding with dense forests. Even with the throng of officers there, it could take days to comb the area. The killer's previous call had contained succinct information. Something didn't feel right. "Where's Kylie?"

"On the other side by the paddock." He tipped his head, gesturing to the area ahead of them. "She's speaking with some of the other media folks."

Nick made his way around the barn. Tension in the air stretched as taut as a trip wire. This old farm, now abandoned, spiraled him back to yesteryear and all the bittersweet memories. He'd grown up with Jake, fished in the nearby streams, climbed every tree within reach and even broken his arm jumping from the hayloft on a dare.

He slanted a glance across the field of wild grasses. A sense of loss and nostalgia flooded him. He could still see Kylie, her eyes glinting beneath the faint moonlight, her dark curls rippling in the breeze.

The first night they'd kissed.

An old ache pulled in his chest, a longing coupled with melancholy and regret.

So many memories.

Two reporters brushed passed him and left Kylie leaning against the remains of an old split-rail fence. Distant police spotlights bathed her in a soft glow.

"You okay?" Nick strode closer.

Kylie's slender shoulders shrugged. "All things considered, I guess. Of course, that will change if another butchered body shows up."

"Not a good thought, huh?"

She shook her head. He found himself looking into the saddest green eyes he'd ever seen.

"Maybe this time the predator was bluffing." Nick preferred to dwell on the positive, though he wouldn't bet on it.

She nodded. "Hope so."

"What exactly did he say?"

She took a moment. "Another gift was waiting for me here."

"Gift? Not body?"

Her face pinched. "No, but his last call didn't specify a body, either. Do you think that matters?"

"Maybe not. But psychopathic minds like order." Nick scratched his jaw, still looking around. "These lunatics plan thoroughly. They thrive on recognition and once they act, they don't like to wait long to get noticed."

Kylie gestured toward the field behind her, teeming with officers and rescue workers. "More chaotic than organized at the moment."

Nick gave a shrug. "Exactly. Did the caller say anything else?"

The wind had a bite now and distant thunder clapped.

"Fireworks. Cows. The moon." Kylie burrowed her hands in her coat pockets. "Random stuff. Although enough to lead me here."

"Random? Maybe. Maybe not." Nick scratched his jaw. His mind was reeling.

"What are you thinking?"

"That there has to be something behind those clues."

"I've always hated riddles," Kylie muttered. She tossed her hair over her shoulder.

"I remember." Nick gave a short chuckle.

The wind kicked up, sighing through the trees; branches snapped and a rusty squeal protested with every gust.

A thought pierced Nick's mind. He took a step back and squinted to see. *Bingo.*

"What are you looking at?"

"Hold on." Nick cupped his mouth and hollered, "Detective Michelson—over here."

A moment later, Dave rounded the corner in a full sprint, with several officers in pursuit. "Do you have something?"

"Hope so." Nick thrust out his hand. "Let me borrow your flashlight."

Dave slapped the Maglite into Nick's palm.

"What is it?" Kylie's question died, only to be replaced by a gasp as Nick focused the light on the barn's roof, illuminating the spinning weather vane. Tarnished and corroded, but without question a tin rendition of a cow over the moon.

In the dimly lit interior of the barn, Kylie leaned against the rough-sided stall and crossed her arms. The plank structure had been constructed near the turn of the century, built solid and strong to last a lifetime. Good thing, because at the moment her ability to stand on her own was sorely in jeopardy.

From across the barn Nick stepped around stacked bales of rotted hay and came to stand beside her. The white glow emitting from his borrowed flashlight brightened the area around them.

"Dave and his officers are on it. They'll catch this creep. Try not to worry, Kylie." Nick's words sounded reassuring, but they did little to reduce her stress.

She nodded.

In the hayloft above them a team of law-enforcement officers combed through the clutter. Just the thought of another murder victim brought chills. Who was this madman?

She lifted a quick prayer. *Lord, protect us and whoever the next victim is.*

At the sound of the rhythmic thump against wooden rungs, Nick took a step and brandished his flashlight toward the loft. Dave clumped his way back down the ladder.

"Anything?" Nick's eager voice echoed back to her.

"Junk. Cobwebs, old lumber, milk buckets, horse tack, a couple old boxes. Dust and more dust." Dave coughed against the back of his hand.

Relaxing a bit, Kylie pushed away from the stall and ambled up beside Nick. "I thank God there wasn't a body." She let go of a long breath.

"Not yet, anyway." Dave joined them, brushing

dirt and dust from his uniform shirt. "The chief just radioed me. They suspended the search for the night. We'll start up again at dawn and get the National Guard out here with us and see what we can find."

Kylie's shoulders tightened again as her mind swung like a pendulum. As much as she hated the idea of stumbling upon another victim, she couldn't fathom leaving any poor soul, alive or dead, undiscovered. "You can't give up looking tonight. I mean, what if—"

"Kylie. It's okay." Nick moved to her. He slipped his strong arm around her and gave her a reassuring hug.

Instinct warned her not to get too close to this man, but before she could stop herself, she sank into the solid wall of his chest.

"Dave's right," Nick continued, his breath feathering warmly against her brow, tenderness and understanding in his tone. "It's dark. And with the weather moving in, finding anything or anyone out there would be impossible. Not to mention we don't even know what we're looking for."

As she burrowed against him, the comfort of his touch surprised Kylie, even scared her, yet at the same time a sensation of security seeped through her like a healing balm. After considering his rationale, she had to agree he was right. But that didn't alleviate her concerns of a casualty lying in wait.

A couple more officers tramped down the ladder, cutting into Kylie's thoughts and bringing clarity to her world.

Pulling away from Nick, Kylie shook off the warmth from his embrace. Years ago she had learned what losing him could do to her heart. She had no plans to go down that path again.

A kick in her chest seemed to object. She hated the way her heart bucked at logic. Squaring her shoulders, she drew fresh air into her lungs, only to inhale the lingering scents of woods, humidity and Nick's spicy cologne. Rubbing her nose, she tried hard not to focus on Nick or how good it had felt to be in his arms again.

"It's been a long day. It will be good for you to get some sleep." Nick's soft voice brought her back.

Absently she nodded, even as a shiver skidded over her skin at the thought of suspending the search. Tomorrow might be too late.

Dave walked off a few yards from them, speaking to the other officers in low tones. Kylie waited beside Nick; although she wasn't intentionally trying to listen, snippets of conversation trickled back to her as the officers talked over plans for the next day.

Her heart tripped when she realized they'd given up on finding anything inside the barn.

"Excuse me, detectives." Her voice escalated

with the pounding of her heart. "You're not ready to give up on the barn already?"

Dave paused and glanced at her beneath the dim lights. "Time is of the essence and we've exhausted this search," he said calmly before turning back to his men.

Kylie took a deep, calming breath. "Do you think they missed anything?" she whispered for just Nick to hear.

He inclined his head and murmured close to her ear, "Even if I did, this is a crime scene and I'm an outsider here. I'm working hard to reserve my opinion and let Dave and his guys do their job. He's already shared more information than he needed to."

She pulled away slightly. "But Dave asked for your help."

"And I'm happy to give it, when he's ready for it. At the moment he's working with his team and I don't want to interfere."

She blinked at him through the dim light. "The clues the caller gave me definitely point to this barn. Maybe if I remind them of that, they'll let us take a quick look around."

Nick's brows pulled together. "You sure you want to do that?"

Kylie nodded with more confidence than she felt. But she agreed with Nick's earlier theory. The caller's cryptic clues probably weren't random. She needed to see, needed to exhaust this search.

"Come on." Her legs went to putty, but determination carried her. She grabbed his hand, surprised by his grip. Firm, tight and undeniably possessive.

She groaned inwardly, pushing aside the illogical nostalgia parading through her.

Dave wasn't as quick to agree as Kylie suspected; in fact he didn't see the point, since they'd scoured the place already. But after a little rationalizing and a lot of insistence, he agreed to accompany them to the hayloft. As he'd described, dust and clutter filled the cramped space. After Mr. and Mrs. Plyler died several years ago, the children had scattered, moving to different parts of the country. They were still fighting over the estate. The hundred-plus acres, including the barn, sat untouched. And it showed.

The high-intensity beams of flashlights cast distorted shadows across the area, adding to the oppressive climate of the evening, which made staying close to Nick a necessity.

"There's nothing up here," Dave grumbled under his breath.

Nick didn't stop his investigation. He pushed aside dangling cobwebs and flashed his light into every nook and cranny. Kylie moved along beside him, although quickly coming to the same conclusion as Dave.

"Look at this." Nick knelt down and directed his light on the side of a small box. *Big Sky Fireworks Company. Sumter, SC.*

He slipped on the latex gloves Dave had given him and looked over at Kylie, his eyes narrowing. "Start taking notes, Reporter Harper. I think we've just hit pay dirt."

Emotion lumped in Kylie's throat. She gave a short nod.

With expert precision, Nick carefully peeled back each flap of the box.

The rush of blood pounding in Kylie's ears merged with the roar of distant thunder. She tried not to jump, tried not to breathe.

Dave came up beside her and glanced over her shoulder. "Looks like nothing more than a bunch of old papers."

Nick picked through the loose pages and pulled a bundle from underneath. "Shine your light over here, Dave."

Dave targeted his flashlight on the bound file in Nick's hands.

Nibbling her lip, Kylie watched carefully as Nick slipped off a rubber band and the bulging folder popped open. Dozens of rough-cut newspaper articles and photos flew into the air before scattering onto the uneven loft floor at Nick's feet.

Setting the empty folder aside, Nick started collecting the documents on the floor.

Kylie gasped and her body went rigid when she realized she was looking at articles she'd written, along with four-by-eight black-and-white prints—of *her*.

# FIVE

Back at the precinct, Nick and Kylie were holed up in the same stuffy room as before, insulated from the rumbling environment outside the door and the local media hounds. Nick sifted through an assortment of photos and clipped newspaper articles. A visual display of Kylie's life over the past ten years.

In one picture, he recognized Kylie's parents and sister, huddled around her at her college graduation. Another caught Kylie handing out drinks at some sort of church event. Other random shots showed her mingling with friends in various settings, some dating back to their high-school years and all taken in public places.

The guy had quite a collection. Nick shook his head and tossed the prints onto the table, the pile beneath it steadily growing. He grabbed the last few from the folder. And as he shuffled through them, surprise kicked his pulse up. One of the pictures was of him and Kylie at their senior prom.

Nick glanced over at Kylie sitting beside him, grateful to find her propped back in her chair reading through the preliminary police report. He doubted she was up for reminiscing.

He added the rest of the photos to the stack, save

one. Sitting back, he indulged himself in a second look at the senior picture.

It was a typical scripted pose, his arm around Kylie's waist, holding her close, their smiles beaming for the camera. She'd looked beautiful that night in her black evening gown. He'd bought her a yellow rose corsage, and she'd given him a matching boutonniere. He'd borrowed his parents' old Cadillac and they ate dinner at Spencer's Steak House, the nicest restaurant in town.

He smiled nostalgically, remembering their first dance. The salsa. A far cry from the country swing they had practiced. He never could figure our who was leading whom. In truth, they'd both worked hard trying to keep from tripping the other.

They'd laughed about it later. He'd promised Kylie that after graduation he'd take ballroom-dance lessons with her.

A bitter sigh caught in his throat. Another promise he hadn't kept.

Nick swallowed twice, dismissing the regret.

Sending Kylie a sidelong glance, he noted how she still looked as youthful as the girl in the picture. And just as beautiful.

His chest once again felt tight. He needed to keep his head on straight. So what if he found Kylie Harper appealing? Aside from that, they were just friends. And that was all they would ever be.

Pages ruffled and Kylie dropped the report on

the table. "All this paperwork and we still don't have a clue on who this predator might be."

Nick blinked, reasserting mental control. He straightened in his seat. "Evidence is building. We're making progress."

Discreetly, he gathered the photos and stuffed them back into the folder.

"I hope so. I'm not really cut out for this." Kylie picked up her coffee and took a drink.

"I don't know about that. You were pretty brave out there today." Nick gave a small chuckle, hoping to lighten the mood. But he couldn't discount the fact that this stalker was no regular predator. He knew too much about Conrad's murder. He had to have been a member of their high-school class. And whoever he was, he'd been harboring ten years of pent-up obsession for Kylie and now he was on the prowl. Couple that with a delusional and brilliant mind and the cops had their job cut out for them.

Kylie slanted him a glance, her lips slightly curved. "Brave? I was shaking in my boots the whole time."

"Fear is a perfectly normal reaction to have in this situation. Pushing past those fears to get a job done makes you…brave." He smiled at her.

She returned it. "Then you were brave. I was tagging along."

Not true, but he wouldn't argue.

"I just keep wondering how I could have missed

someone stalking me." Kylie set her cup on the table, the coffee almost spilling.

"Psychopaths like this guy can be elusive. It's part of the game, Kylie. Part of the sickness." Nick reached over to capture her hand and steady her cup, steady her.

"What kind of creep collects ten years' worth of pictures, plus every published article I've written, and doesn't make himself known?" Kylie's voice drifted off, as if she were trying to make sense of it all. She pulled her hand away, and the warmth inside him took on a chill as she thumped back in the chair and crossed her arms.

Nick gave a slight shrug. "Someone obsessed, that's who. It doesn't have to make sense when someone is crazy."

She shook her head, her gaze never leaving his face. "Well, it doesn't make sense. An average girl. A small-town reporter. Hardly a person of celebrity status."

"First of all, Miss Harper." He leaned in closer, lifted a brow. "You are far from average. Always have been."

"Really?"

Her amused laugh pricked his heart. For the better part of his teenage years he'd been in love with this woman. Beyond her gentle beauty, she was curious and funny. And the simple moments they'd spent together still warmed him to the core. Impromptu picnics along the parkway, long walks, hiking, even playing board games on a cold winter's day.

He breathed deeply and smiled. "Yes, Kylie Harper. You are far from average."

"That's sweet of you to say." She picked up her cup and took another sip of coffee.

"I'm serious. I've never met anyone else like you."

Kylie lowered her cup, all the humor erased from her expression. "Then why did you leave, Nick? And forget all about me?"

"I…" Straightening, Nick stammered. He hadn't been prepared for that.

"I'm sorry. That wasn't fair—" Kylie's voice broke.

The slash in Nick's heart widened. Only a wimp would abandon a woman like this. He'd managed to accomplish the one thing he'd promised he'd never do—hurt Kylie Harper. And apparently he was still doing so.

He shook his head. "No, you asked a perfectly good question. One I've asked myself dozens of times over the years. Honestly, Kylie, I could never forget you. And although guilt and anger played a heavy part in my decision to leave, it was time for me to move on. Still, I should have discussed it with you. I shouldn't have turned my back on you like I did."

"Don't." She waved a dismissive hand. "Please,

no explanation. We had already broken up. You owed me nothing."

How wrong she was. Nick wasn't about to leave that misconception hanging. "Kylie—" He looked into her eyes, but her gaze swung beyond his shoulder toward the glass door behind him as it squeaked open.

"Have you found anything interesting?" Kylie's eyebrows lifted and her hopeful tone bumped up a notch.

"Not yet." Dave shuffled into the room. He removed the stack of files from a chair and dropped into it. "We're still waiting to hear back from the lab. They're looking over the evidence gathered at the scene. We should have a report by morning."

"What is the probability of a fingerprint match?" Kylie divided her hopeful glance between Nick and Dave.

"Slim." Dave beat Nick to the punch.

"Sorry, Kylie." Nick folded his arms across his chest before he gave in to the urge to reach over to comfort her again. He'd roused enough old feelings…for both of them. "The box was obviously planted for us to find. This guy isn't going to be careless."

"That's right." Dave grunted in agreement.

"And what about suspects?" Nick met Dave's weary gaze.

"At the moment, everyone in our graduating class is on our list."

Nick nodded. "Good, I was hoping you'd start there."

Kylie kneaded her hand across her forehead, pushing it back into her hair. "I don't know what to do. Leave town. Get a hotel room."

A problem Nick could help her with. "My brother's house. Remember? His guest room awaits. I'm next door in the apartment above the store."

"Then again—" Kylie tipped her head and he could just about see the wheels turning. "It doesn't seem very logical that the killer would come anywhere near my house. He knows the police are anticipating his next move. I'm sure I'll be safe."

*Denial or stubbornness?* Nick bet on the latter. That hadn't changed. Nick took a deep breath. "We're not talking about someone with a rational mind. You shouldn't be taking chances."

"But—"

"It wouldn't hurt to be cautious," Dave ground out.

Kylie's eyes skittered back to Dave. "Can't you have an officer patrol my street?"

A frown puckered Dave's brow as he stared back at her, a heavy silence weighting the air around them. "Not often enough to guarantee your safety. Besides, you're pretty isolated where you live."

Kylie pushed her chair away from the table and stood. "Well, then, I guess I don't have much choice." She pulled her handbag from the back of the chair. "Nick, if you don't mind accompanying me to my house to pick up a few things, I'll take you up on your offer. That is, if you're sure."

"Absolutely." Nick wanted to say more. Something to make her more comfortable about the new living arrangements. He knew what she was thinking: being thrown together was going to be awkward for both of them.

Nothing encouraging came to mind. Still, he was glad she hadn't resisted staying so close to him. It made keeping up with her easier. Whether Nick liked it or not, he was knee-deep in this mess with her, and he vowed to be her shadow.

"I guess we should get going." Kylie stepped toward the door, her words pulling him out of his meandering thoughts.

Nick got to his feet and headed out behind her. After three tours in the Middle East, he understood fear. At times it even consumed him, gripping him to the bone. But now, with a madman after Kylie, *fear* took on a whole new meaning.

Nick led Kylie in through the side door of his brother's older clapboard bungalow. There was a small table and chairs in a kitchen and the faint smell of rotting fruit hung in the air.

"Sorry." He set her suitcase by the door and turned on the overhead fan. "I stopped by earlier and realized that food needed to be thrown away." Thankfully, they'd stopped for takeout on the way.

"Not a problem." Kylie smiled weakly and sank onto one of the chairs. A lock of rain-drizzled hair dangled across her cheek and her eyes looked weary.

Nick dropped the bag of burgers on the table. He flexed his fingers and prayed she'd brush the wisp aside before he gave in to his urge and did it himself. *Keep your head straight,* he ordered himself, then breathed relief when Kylie looped the stray curl behind her ear.

"Can I get you anything to drink?" Nick wrestled off his jacket and hung it on the hook by the door.

"No, thanks. This water is fine." She sipped from the straw in her paper cup.

Nick tore open the bag and pulled out the contents. He held up three burgers and a large pack of fries. "A feast meant for a king…and queen." He grinned.

She chuckled and took one of the burgers. "Thanks."

Kylie bowed her head in a moment of silence. "Lord, bless this food to our body. In Your blessed name, Amen."

"And watch over Kylie and keep her safe," Nick added. He couldn't remember the last time he'd said a prayer. But if ever there was a need, this was the time.

Eyes as green as precious emeralds met his, bumping his pulse up a notch. "Thank you, Nick."

"You're welcome." Nick dropped his gaze and bit into a fry. "Just wanted to add my two cents, in case He was listening."

"Well, He's always listening. But I'm not thanking you just for the prayer. I'd like to thank you for everything. You know you don't have to do this."

"Do what?" He wiped French-fry salt off his fingers.

A gentle smile lifted the corner of her lips. "Get involved in this mayhem."

"Too late." He grinned. "Besides, that's what friends are for." The moment the word *friend* popped out, Nick wished it back. Even after all this time, *friend* didn't seem appropriate. And by the grimace on Kylie's face, she agreed.

"If this guy happens to be Conrad's killer, I want to be in the mix and help bring that creep down," he amended. On the tail end of that thought he added, "And of course, help ensure your safety."

Nick clamped his mouth shut. He was beginning to sound like some wannabe superhero instead of Kylie's old boyfriend who cared about her safety.

After a moment, her expression relaxed and she nodded. "Thank you, it is good to have friends."

And a fine friend he'd been. He'd been out of her life for years. Plenty of times he'd almost caved in and contacted her. Fortunately, logic had overridden impulse. The top secret missions and foreign-defense operations kept him out of touch for months on end. And there was no guarantee where he'd end up next.

Even if they had rekindled their relationship, he couldn't have expected her to put her life on hold, only to worry about where he was or what he was involved in. Or worse, wonder if he would make it home.

Too many of his comrades didn't return, and out of those who did, many ended up divorced. A lose-lose situation, he'd decided.

He took a swig of his drink to cover his sigh.

Besides, he would never have gotten Kylie out of Asheville. And the thought of coming back to make a home and a life here had made his skin crawl.

Nope, better he never made the call. Besides, they had too much history and hurt between them.

Still, her sweet spirit and beauty tugged at his heart, which made being around her that much harder. He had no intention of staying in town long-term and his future plans were as unpredictable as an ice storm in July.

She deserved better. Much more than he could offer.

Later that same evening, Kylie curled beneath the down comforter in Steven's guest room as raindrops tinked against the window and gusts of wind moaned a lazy serenade. A perfect backdrop for a good night's sleep, had her mind not been racing, consumed by the hows and the whys of the case. A futile venture. Nonetheless, she couldn't let go of one nagging thought: for the stalker to have a photo anthology of her the way he did, he had to live in Asheville and she obviously knew him.

Someone discreet, ordinary and inconspicuous.

Those characteristics described almost anyone in her social circle or workplace. Adding *malicious* or *dangerous* to the list didn't cause a hint of revelation.

With a sigh, she sat up, plumped her pillow and lay back down, resting one arm behind her head. She stared into the darkness, confident of the Lord's presence, yet fearful that at any moment her cell phone would ring and the nightmare would begin again.

Rolling to her side, she picked up her cell, which had been charging on the lamp table, and checked her phone log. No missed calls, which suited her fine. She placed it back on the table before she gave in to the temptation to switch it to vibrate and forget about Dave's request for her to keep her phone turned on and accessible. Since this stalker seemed driven to gain her attention, everyone investigating the case expected him to call.

In truth, so did she.

Kylie yanked the blankets to her chin, warding off the chill that the thought brought. Closing her eyes, she started to pray. After endless moments, a cozy warmth wrapped around her, a welcome reprieve.

Hours later, somewhere between somnolence and slumber, a vigorous ring punctuated her foggy consciousness.

Kylie jerked up and pulled away from the warmth of her bed. Disoriented and breathing rapidly, she glanced around, clutching the thin bedsheet to her chest, wondering if she was awake or still dreaming.

The soft light of dawn streamed through the sheer window covering. She blinked and caught her breath, grappling to catch up, focus. Even as her thoughts became more lucid, all she wanted to do was sink back down and snuggle beneath the blankets.

The brisk ring came again, awakening her fully.

Her pulse sprinted. Fears came tumbling back, of death and stalkers, a perpetrator on the loose.

Was that him now?

The very thought made it hard for her to breathe. She snatched up her cell phone and checked the display. *Restricted* flashed across the screen.

Closing her eyes, she pressed the cell to her ear. *Ready.* She had to be ready. "Hello." She cleared her voice. A prayer caught in her throat. *Lord, help me.*

"Kylie. Are you up?"

With a rapid exhale, Kylie crumpled against the headboard. "Max, you scared me to death."

A hearty chuckle. "Not quite to death."

"Close enough. Why is your phone coming up restricted?"

"It's my personal line at home. Sorry to call so early, but I wanted to get the lowdown on last night."

"Last night? Didn't you get a copy of the article I sent to the managing editor?"

"Of course. Headline news. Front and center on the morning press. But I wanted to know the behind-the-scenes story. Who do you suspect?"

Kylie rubbed at her forehead, the evident birth of a major headache. "No one."

"Come on. You have to suspect someone. Ten years' worth of pictures?"

"And every published article I've written."

"Creepy."

"Very much so."

A pause. Max at a loss for words? Impossible. Finally "And you suspect no one?"

Kylie sighed, rubbing her head harder. "Nada."

"Well, then, kiddo, dig deep and think about it. Keep me posted when you hear from that psychopath again."

She shuddered. "Maybe he won't call again. Maybe he's had enough fun for another ten years?"

"You want this monster on the loose for another ten years?"

She didn't want him loose for another ten seconds. "Of course not."

"The cops installed a tracking device on your phone, didn't they?"

"They did."

"Then let's pray he calls."

"Sure, Max."

Max hung up and Kylie tapped the cell phone against her chin. He was right, of course, but that didn't make waiting for a crazy man's call any easier.

She slipped back under her blankets, snuggled into a comfortable position and had just closed her eyes when a thumping noise caught her attention. Her heart stalled and her eyes popped open. She waited, completely frozen, as she listened.

A distant deep, gravelly voice rumbled from somewhere in the house. Shooting up in bed, she squinted at the digital display on her cell phone. Five forty-five. Would Nick be up this early? And talking on the phone to someone? Stiffening, she strained her ears to detect any movements over the moan of the gusty wind outside the window. For seconds nothing, then soft clumps and a thud sounded.

She remembered Nick saying he'd see her at seven. Schooling herself to stay calm, she switched on the bedside lamp. The bulb flickered on, chasing shadows into the far corners of the room. She breathed easier.

Silence lingered for another ten seconds, then floorboards creaked, sending her stomach plunging. Her calm evaporated. As she cocked her head, her ears picked up a raspy mumble. Definitely a voice. Someone was in the house.

Icy fingers stroked along her spine, setting off an epidemic of goose bumps.

As she rubbed at the raised patches on her arms, wind gusts rattled the outside shutters. Fear dissolved into relief. It must have only been the wind.

But when something hard struck the floor, she kicked back her covers and clambered to her feet, her phone dropping to the floor.

Grabbing her robe from the back of a chair, she quickly pulled it on. Her eyes went to the door. Darkness seeped through the cracks around the edges of the jamb. If Nick was out there, wouldn't he turn on the lights?

Another bump startled her into action. She started to call out to him and then clamped a hand over her lips. What if it wasn't Nick?

Nerves on alert, she rushed to the door. She slipped her fingers over the knob, ready to punch in the lock. Firm footsteps hit the rustic hardwood in the hallway and she retracted her hand. The steady booted clip sent a shudder of fear ripping through her.

Frozen in place, she counted the long seconds until the plodding steps halted, right outside her bedroom door.

Fighting down the shriek that had risen in her throat, she tried for the doorknob again and her fingers fumbled at the first attempt. Then taking a deep breath, she managed to lock it.

Relief trickled through her.

Now she needed her phone, needed to text Nick, that is, if she could only get her legs to move and stop trembling.

The air around her went still and the footsteps started again.

She released a breath and strained to listen.

Hinges creaked. A door banged.

Shivering, she pivoted around and sagged against the closed door, working to breathe. Working to think.

A shadowed movement caught her eye outside the window. Wind howled, leaves rustled, a tree branch crackled, tediously tapping against the glass pane.

*The gusty breeze.* She held her breath, hoping that was all.

Seconds passed. A dark silhouette of a man emerged, hurrying by the window.

Her mouth dropped open, but she quickly recovered, avoiding a gasp. Pushing fear aside, she scooted across the room to the window and tugged back a corner of the curtain. She peered intently through the pane, lifting her gaze above the top of the bushes. No one was there. Nothing looked out of the ordinary.

Just when she was convinced she was going crazy, a car spun past the house, red taillights burning through the morning fog. She dropped to the floor and scrambled on her knees to her cell phone.

Confusion merged with the anxiety twisting away at her insides. What was going on? Was she now alone? Or would someone at any moment knock down the door and find her?

Staying silent, she frantically scrolled through her contacts and typed Nick a message—HELP!

# SIX

Facing the mirror in the bathroom, Nick stopped shaving his morning stubble when a text alert sounded on his cell.

Only a few people had his number. And that scared him.

Fumbling with the razor in his hand, he lost his grip, sending it clanking against the porcelain sink, but not before the sharp edge of the blade nicked him.

With the back of his hand, he swiped a dribble of blood from his chin and then lifted his phone off the sink basin. His heart tripped as he glared at the one-word text from Kylie.

HELP!

Snatching his keys, he wrestled on a pair of jogging pants and T-shirt as he made his way out of the small apartment. Taking two steps at a time, he bounded down a short flight of steps and crossed the driveway into the neighboring yard. He plunged his key into the lock of the side-porch door. A moment later, he was in the kitchen. Silence greeted him.

*Stay calm.* He held his tongue. Didn't call out.

Senses on alert, Nick moved from one room to the next, his heart beating wildly despite his best efforts to stay rational. His combat-mission training had taught him to focus, carefully process the situation and then act.

No emotion involved. Something he'd perfected—until today.

A chill lingered in the air and the house was quiet. Nothing looked out of the ordinary, except the closed door to Kylie's room.

He posed a hard-knuckled knock against the wood. "Kylie, are you okay?"

A sigh or a whimper. He couldn't be sure.

Gripping the handle, he firmly leaned a shoulder against the door, ready to break it down if necessary. "Kylie," he called out again.

"Nick!" Kylie's panicked voice answered him.

The knob rattled a second before the door whipped open. He gripped the doorframe and righted his stance to keep from toppling onto her.

"There was someone in the house. He was in the hall, right outside my door," she rasped out.

Questions and urgency flooded Nick's thoughts.

Kylie eased toward him, trembling. Shock and fear tightened her features. She didn't look capable of staying on her feet, much less supplying him with the answers he needed.

"Let's get you to a chair and then you can tell me everything." He draped an arm around her, steadying her.

Her slender frame compressed against him and wisps of her silky hair tickled his cheek. He tried to ignore the awareness it brought. Instinctively, he pulled her closer and guided her down the wood-floored hall until they emerged into the kitchen. He settled her into a chair and flipped on the light.

Kylie's chest heaved with audible breaths. She expelled a raspy sigh, her trembling fingers clutching her cell phone.

He hunkered down in front of her and gave her a moment to recover.

"It's okay." He spoke softly, brushing errant locks from her face. And as he peered at her, the temptation to pull her close and comfort her burned deep inside him. Inhaling slowly, he bridled the emotion.

"It had to be him," she muttered after a moment.

"Who are we talking about, Kylie?"

"The perpetrator. The killer. The stalker. Whoever he is."

"Did you see someone?"

She shook her head. "No, but I heard him. He walked past my room. Then he went outside, I think through the front door." She put a hand on Nick's arm; her eyes widened. "And there was a crash. Something heavy fell on the floor."

"Heavy? Like a pan or glass?"

She wagged her head. "Something solid. Maybe a gun or flashlight."

That thought brought Nick to his feet. "Wait

here." He walked out of the kitchen and into the living room. He scanned the area and then went from there to each of the other rooms in the house, looking for any signs of an intruder. As before, nothing was out of place. The front and back doors remained locked, as were the windows.

Paranoia and fear, he hoped, were the culprits. Breathing easier, Nick circled back to the kitchen. "Everything looks okay. The windows and doors are secure."

Kylie's head shot up. "Then how would some-one get in?"

"Well, maybe what you heard wasn't *someone*. There are all sorts of creaks and noises in this old house."

"No, I heard footsteps, a man's voice."

"The wind, blowing trees, even distant traffic can sound distorted."

"But he ran past my window. And I saw his car—"

Nick cut her off. "You saw a man?"

Kylie's heart was sinking fast. "Well, actually, more like a shadow."

"And a car? What kind?"

"I don't know." She gave a quick shrug. "Just a car. It was racing down the street...." Her words trailed off.

Silence fell between them, along with a sudden chill that crept into her bones. Now she wasn't sure about anything.

Kylie stared at him for a moment. Then with a sigh, she dragged her fingers through her tousled curls. "You think I'm crazy, don't you?"

Nick shook his head. "No, I think you're scared. You have every right to be. I'm not discounting what you heard. You may be right, someone may have been inside the house. Although I hope not."

Kylie got to her feet, swallowed visibly. "I hope not, too."

Right then, Nick's heart shattered along with the protective wall he'd erected between them. He gathered her in his arms, held her tight. She needed his comfort, and like it or not, he needed hers.

The tension between Kylie's shoulders slowly abated. She leaned deep into Nick's embrace, savoring his tender touch. Instead of fear, warmth and safety trickled through her. She felt safe in his arms. Dangerous. He'd broken her heart once. She needed to remember that, keep her thoughts in perspective. But for now, that worry would have to wait.

She glanced up at him, conscious of his attentive gaze, soulful brown eyes blazing with concern. A hint of a grimace stretched across his jaw. She blinked, noticing for the first time the bloody gash on his chin.

She broke loose from his grip. "Nick, you're bleeding."

He ran a finger across his half-stubbled chin. "I guess the razor got the best of me this morning."

"More likely my text got the best of you. I feel terrible." Kylie turned and hurried to the cabinet. From a small basket near the sink, she grabbed a napkin, feeling foolish for overreacting. She turned back.

"No worries. I'm fine, really." Nick's voice trailed off as he cast a curious glance at something on the floor. Crouching, he reached under the table and palmed something in his hand.

"What is it?"

"Probably nothing." Nick stood upright and between his fingers he clutched a sheet of paper folded into a small rectangle. He opened it and started to read the note.

Seconds ticked by and the weight of concern strangling her chest pulled even tighter when the muscles in Nick's jaw visibly tightened. Her breath caught.

"Nick?"

He glanced up, a dire expression on his face. "I don't like this."

Struggling to control her rising fear, Kylie sidled up beside him and stared at the words. One scribbled sentence: *Never more than a heartbeat away.*

Her heart stopped.

At Steven's kitchen table, Kylie sat bundled in her bathrobe, cupping a mug in her hands. Barely eight in the morning and her day had escalated from rocky to rotten.

"Okay, Kylie. Let's get back to the make and color of the car you saw speeding by the house this morning."

Before she could explain to Dave for the umpteenth time that the fog and gray skies made identifying the car impossible, the front door swung open and another uniformed officer walked into the house. He joined the others already combing through the rooms, taking down notes and dusting for fingerprints.

A pointless venture. Kylie sighed. Nick's words from the day before resonated in her head. *This guy isn't going to be careless.*

Whoever this madman was, he'd planted the note. Along with the pictures and the body at the airport. He wanted them found. Wanted her scared.

She shivered with a sigh.

Accolades to him. He had succeeded in doing just that.

"Kylie." Dave pulled out a chair and sat beside her. "Do you have any idea of who this guy might be?"

"Believe me, Dave, I've racked my brain over and over again. Unfortunately, I keep coming up with the same thing."

He quirked a brow.

"Nothing."

His thick, bushy brows dropped flat like a slash

over his eyes. "Okay, then make me a list of old boyfriends. Long relationships, short, it doesn't matter."

That was an easy assignment. Kylie gestured with her cup toward Nick. "There you go."

Nick straightened from his slouch at the counter, his brows lifted. "I'm not sure how to take that. Was I that bad of a boyfriend that you were afraid to try again, or have I just been too hard to replace?" A chuckle underscored his words and Kylie wasn't about to go there.

At least not today.

She set her cup down with a clink and shrugged. "College kept me busy. And now, between work and church activities, I don't have time for a relationship."

Kylie fought not to cringe. That sounded lame even to her own ears.

"Right," Dave grunted. He eyed her for a split second, then tossed a notepad and pen on the table. "Make me a list of the men that have showed some interest in you. Maybe you brushed one of them off, offended them somehow. Consider your circle of friends, neighbors, online buddies, even coworkers."

"Men that I've known for the last ten years?"

"Time frame doesn't matter. Criminals like this can be resourceful when something intrigues them."

Kylie brushed hair from her face. "You're asking me to remember everyone who ever made a pass at me?" As a journalist, she had met and mingled with men in all lines of work all over the area. Flirting wasn't unusual, nor was an invitation to meet them for dinner or a drink. "No, thanks" was her common reply. She never mixed business with pleasure.

Nick whistled softly between his teeth. "Must be a bunch." He leaned a shoulder against the side of the kitchen cupboards and crossed his arms.

The smirk on his face brought a warm flush to her cheeks. This man was too cute for his own good—and hers. She took the last swig of cold tea, hoping he couldn't read her mind or her heart.

She needed to get a grip, plain and simple. But having Nick around triggered a host of emotions. At the moment those feelings overrode logic.

"Do your best, Kylie. We have to start somewhere." Dave gave the table a firm slap before he pushed back his chair and stood.

"I'll try, Dave. Thanks for all your—"

The brisk ring of a cell phone stopped Kylie midsentence. Her heart lurched. Irrational fear coursed through every vessel.

Dave retrieved his phone from his belt clip and pressed it to his ear. "Detective Dave Michelson here."

A short conversation ensued, the gist of which eluded Kylie.

"Thanks, I appreciate the information." Dave

snapped his phone off. A frown drifted across his features.

"That was Tom Walden at the coroner's office. Preliminary autopsy reports are in on the first victim."

"And what did they find?" Kylie straightened.

Dave shifted his weight and slid his cell into his phone holster. "It seems that on the night of Tucker's murder, he was quite intoxicated. In fact, his blood-alcohol level was five times the legal limit."

"Five times?" Kylie echoed. "How would he even function?"

"Good question," Nick piped up. "In fact, he probably couldn't. He may not have even been conscious when he was killed. Isn't that correct, Detective?"

Dave tilted his head, gave a shrug. "That's possible."

"An easy target." Nick shook his head. "This kind of creep preys on the helpless."

"Helpless? I hope that's not what he thinks I am," Kylie muttered, more to herself than to anyone else, trying to make sense of it all.

A grimace took hold of Nick's lips. "No. It's more personal than that. You've somehow captured his attention."

"Wonderful." She sighed.

She'd only ever wanted one man's attention. And right now his dark liquid eyes held hers. A prickly heat rose up her neck. Shaking it off, she smoothed her robe, inhaling deeply.

Kylie was beginning to wonder what scared her more: a psychopathic stalker or the allure of Nick Bentley.

At the moment her heart banked on the latter.

Blowing out a long breath, Kylie worked to sweep lingering regrets and sorrow aside.

Picking up the pen Dave gave her, she jotted some notes on the pad. If nothing else, Max would expect an article from her for the evening edition. No better time to start than the present.

Then she remembered something. She stopped writing, looked up and caught Dave's gaze. "What came up on the phone tracer from yesterday's call?"

"A pay phone on Aberdene Street. Officers scoured the area, interviewed the locals, but found nothing."

"Pay phone? But the number came up restricted, like a cell—"

Swiftly, Dave cut her off. "Pay phones show up that way. The phone company wants calls going out, not coming in."

Disappointment pulsed in her veins. "The guy's pretty smart."

Dave shrugged. "We knew it was a long shot. But we'll keep the wire on. Anyway, think about what we talked about and let me know when you come up with some names."

She nodded as he pulled his radio from his belt and headed out the door.

"So, a whole slew of love interests, but no serious boyfriends since we broke up?" Nick settled in the seat beside her, giving her a dubious look.

Hesitating, Kylie stared into the masculine face she remembered so well. His strong jawline and the hint of the smile stretched across it brought her back.

Once she'd known him better than anyone. Now he was as mysterious as any first date. And answering a question like that, well…talk about social suicide. The truth seemed too simple. Too lonely.

Especially compared to his lively career. A Special Forces soldier. Strong. Gorgeous. Women everywhere probably flocked to him.

Kylie picked up her cup, curling her hand around it. What was the point of trying to fluff up her love life? She had no reason to compete. She caught his eye, feigning nonchalance. "Nope, no serious boyfriends since we broke up."

Nick narrowed his gaze slightly. "I hope it wasn't because of me. I know I left you hanging."

Kylie held up a hand, halting the direction the conversation was heading and protecting her heart at the same time.

"Nick, we were kids. No guilt, okay?"

"Well, I should have handled things differently

and I'm sorry," he said in a low voice, regret in his tone.

Her heart squeezed, but she managed a smile. "Me, too."

# SEVEN

The next day, Nick inhaled a long breath and rang up the last few items for the customer in line, thankful that the morning rush at the store was letting up.

"Thank you, ma'am. Have a good day." He manufactured a smile and handed the patron her two bags.

The older woman nodded and made her way to the exit.

Nick eased back against the counter and glanced around, eyeballing the few milling customers that were left. No one seemed to need his attention.

Good. He needed a little reprieve.

Even when he'd worked at the store with his father as a kid, he'd dreaded his time at the register. Not that he preferred to be lazing around. Give him an ax and some logs and he'd chop and stack wood all day. Unlike Steven, who was into the business end of things, which had worked out pretty well for his family.

Nick crossed his arms and let go of a breath, air whistling through his teeth.

He'd always felt claustrophobic being cooped up in the store. A phenomenon his parents hadn't given much credence to.

But here he was ten years later and that claustrophobic feeling was back; the room was closing in on him while fresh air was being sucked out. He gulped a breath. He was ready to be out of this place.

With the turmoil about Kylie clogging every brain cell, the sooner he got out of there, the better.

He glanced at his watch. Almost noon. He'd called Roger, one of the salesclerks, to come in early. Hopefully, he'd remembered.

Even before Nick completely finished the thought, the bell on the front door jangled and Roger walked in.

Just in time. Standing upright, Nick untied his shop apron and tossed it under the register. He worked his way around the counter, giving the employee a firm pat on the shoulder as he made his way to the exit. "Thanks, Roger. There will be a bonus in your paycheck for this."

"Hey, no problem. And thanks for the extra bucks." The clatter of the bell punctuated Roger's words as Nick walked out the century-old door.

He couldn't pay Roger enough.

Thankfully, his brother didn't mind him taking some time to be with Kylie. He seemed rather intrigued, in fact. Steven was probably surmising that something might rekindle between them. But after all this time, that wasn't going to happen.

Sorrow settled in Nick's chest. Bad memories died hard, and so did regret.

In the few days since he'd arrived, every recollection he wanted to erase from his life had seemed to slap him in the face. Conrad's death still pricked at his heart like a rusty nail. And now Kylie reignited memories that he'd carefully kept hidden.

If that wasn't enough, Kylie was in danger. Anger welled up in his chest at the thought. He hated to even consider how much torment the stalker had planned before he physically harmed her.

Something Nick wasn't going to let happen.

That notion started out as a plan and quickly bumped up to determination, giving him an adrenaline rush. Picking up his stride, he wove his way through the tightly packed parking area until he spotted his brother's motorcycle.

He stood there a moment and scratched his chin.

The back tire was low. He'd probably hit a rock or nail on that rough road to Jake Plyler's Barn. He made a mental note to stop by the gas station and have it checked out. One more thing on his overflowing list of things he had to get done today.

Lunch first, he reminded himself as he fished keys from his front pocket.

Nick swung onto the seat and started the cycle. Forty minutes later, he pulled into a parking spot at the *Asheville Daily News*. He'd promised Kylie he'd be there by one. He checked his watch—right on time. He secured his helmet on the back of the seat and pulled a bag and two canned drinks from the side pouch. Not an easy feat, stopping to pick up lunch and getting it to the destination uncrushed. Steven obviously hadn't thought out that scenario when he purchased a motorcycle as his primary mode of transportation. Then again, bicycle riding hadn't proved any better.

Nick smiled at the thought of his brother holed up in the hospital with one leg in traction. A motorcycle spill could have been lethal. He'd have to remind his brother of that. A Hummer or a tank might prove to be a safer bet.

As Nick neared Kylie's desk, she looked up.

"Lunch." He lifted a crinkled bag.

"Great. Do you mind if we eat inside? I'm waiting on my edits."

"Sure."

Grabbing a spare chair, he pulled it beside hers. He waited as she cleared a spot on her desk and spread a page from the newspaper on top.

"Recycled, but clean." She inclined her head and smiled.

An impromptu picnic. Ah, so Kylie. He settled in the chair and handed her a soda.

She popped the lid. "Smells good. Kind of rich and tangy. What did you bring?"

Nick opened the bag. He glanced in and shook his head. "It started as barbecued grilled-chicken sandwiches and chips. Now I believe we have chicken flatbread and potato crumbs."

"Umm. Sounds good." She laughed.

"Still game for an adventure, I see." He removed her lunch from the bag and handed it to her.

She accepted his offering and arranged it on the desk in front of her.

"That was one of the things I used to love about you. You never were afraid of trying new things."

She broke eye contact with him and took a bite of her sandwich, but not before he saw her gaze turn stormy.

Nick nearly choked on the bite he'd taken. *Love.* Why'd he have to say that? Let alone *used* to love. *Open mouth, insert foot.* Size thirteen, at that.

"I'm glad you still have an inquisitive spirit. It's nice that some things don't change." He tried for clarification to make amends.

"I've changed plenty, Nick."

"Oh?" Now he was curious.

She took another bite, and he did also.

"So." He swallowed. "What changes have you made?"

"Well," she muttered, dabbing the sides of her mouth, "I'm more routine and settled. Not quite as impulsive as when I was younger. And, yes—" she met his gaze, her eyes focused on his "—it is awkward when you use the word *love.* Especially in the past tense."

The woman could read his mind. That hadn't changed.

"Sorry. I'll try to watch my words."

She lowered her lashes, hiding her expression. "Thank you."

He took a bite of his sandwich, chastising himself for his poor choice of words.

"I just don't like to be reminded of my mistakes." She finished her statement with a sigh and Nick bit his tongue to keep from choking. Mistake?

*Ouch.* That hurt, in more ways than one.

Nick sat there a moment, mulling over a response for a comment like that. True, their relationship hadn't worked out, but he'd never considered it a mistake. A growing experience, maybe. Could she really believe it was anything other than that? Or was she just trying to get back at him?

No. That didn't sound like Kylie. She was too sweet.

Taking another bite, he didn't bother to try to figure out her motives. His years of training in psychological criminology had supplied him with insight into the behavior and mental processes of the criminal mind. But when it came to the mind of a woman, he was still at a loss.

Nick wadded up the sandwich wrapper and tossed it into the trash. He'd let the *mistake* comment ride for the moment. For now he had more important tasks to attend to.

Catching a stalker was number one on his list.

\* \* \*

An awkward quietness lapsed between them.

Setting her canned drink on her desk, Kylie shot a quick glance at Nick from beneath her lashes. The bewilderment that had momentarily captured his features was displaced by a cool and relaxed expression.

The poor man was probably confused by her sensitivity to their past. Obviously it wasn't something he dwelled on.

Kylie raised her drink to her lips again and took another sip. The logical part of her brain shouted, *Good for him.* But emotionally, her heart slipped a little.

"By the way, I had a nice conversation with Dave today." Nick finally spoke after chasing his last bite of chips down with a drink of cola.

"He gave me permission to look over the facts in the case," Nick continued, wiping his fingers with a paper napkin. "I plan to compile them on a flowchart and see how the pieces fit together."

She glanced at him, impressed. "You sound so organized."

The glint of fervor in his eyes impressed her even more. "It's helps to write things down and study them on paper. I call it my investigative road map. Hopefully, the trail of clues on that map will lead us to your stalker."

"Sounds like a great plan." She nodded.

Nick displayed the dedication and zeal he'd had

when he was young. A man of integrity who had a passion to fix what was broken, lend a helping hand and not let anyone down. Although it was an impossible quest to live up to, as it turned out.

The precarious situation she'd put him in the night Conrad was killed still haunted her.

With a plan to capture a panoramic view of the campsite at sunset for the yearbook, she'd coerced Nick into sneaking away from camp and coming along, knowing he wouldn't let her go alone. Though the trek took longer than either of them had expected, she'd still selfishly pushed forward, not concerned enough about getting back before curfew.

If her youthful judgment hadn't been skewed, maybe Nick's presence would have diverted the killer and spared Conrad's life.

She and Nick had pondered that question for days after the murder. It was no surprise that Nick had ended up fighting for his country, involved in the most deadly missions on earth. Penance.

And her wrenching penance: a life without him.

Kylie had played by the rules all her life, but one slipup had cost her everything.

*Stop it!* She swallowed a sigh along with her bite. She'd rehashed enough. Besides, who was to say the outcome would have been different even if Nick had been there?

Acid burned in her stomach and made eating

impossible. She wadded up the last of her sandwich in its wrapper.

From the corner of her eye, she caught Nick's skeptical gaze.

"Are you okay?"

Kylie hesitated, then shrugged, twisting in her chair to face him. "Fine. Just thinking."

"The last few days have been pretty scary. I'm sure you have a lot on your mind."

Much more than he could imagine. She wiped her hands. "I'm coming along. I'm not too worried. I'm trying just to trust in the Lord."

Nick nodded, appearing to buy into her comment, but the strain in his eyes told her differently.

He, too, was worried.

Warmth trickled through her knowing he still cared. Then she came to her senses.

Beyond Nick's caring disposition, he was a master of intelligence, trained to take on hijackers, terrorists and serial killers. He'd stumbled into this mess, and being who he was, he couldn't walk away. He was doing his job. Doing what he did best.

She was only extraneous baggage.

Gathering herself, she shoved away the troubling thoughts and got back to business.

"Beyond collecting clues, what are we going to do about this maniac?"

Nick laughed and the tension in the room dissolved some. "Believe me, I have plenty of ideas on what to do with this creep once he's caught. But a bigger question still remains—who is he?"

"That's what we need to find out before law enforcement does. We have exclusive rights to this story and we need to hold on to them," a deep voice rumbled from behind her.

Kylie knew the culprit even before she shot a glance over her shoulder and locked her gaze on Max.

"My life is in danger and you're worried about an exclusive?"

A slow grin cracked his lips as he made his way to her from the doorway. "Safety first, of course. Still, keep an investigative mind. Don't push the creep away—draw him in. And once all the facts are in and the culprit is exposed, you'll need to pounce on the story before our competition does."

Nick shot her an unamused look and Kylie breathed easier. She recognized that expression and it wasn't a passive one. Settling back in her seat, she decided to let him take it from there.

"What are you thinking? This is some sort of James Bond adventure flick?" Nick fried Max with a glare. "There's a lunatic on the loose. When this thing finally ends and the credits roll, I don't care who has the exclusive."

Max grinned and walked toward Nick. He thrust out his hand. "I'm Max Dawson, chief editor and Kylie's boss. You must be Nick Bentley."

Nick rose from his seat and shook his hand, not impressed.

"Kylie told me you were in town. I remember the article she wrote about you a few years back. You have quite a résumé." Max fell back a step and draped his lanky frame along the edge of a desk. He crossed his arms.

"Article?" Nick's glance flicked to Kylie.

A rush of bright pink invaded her cheeks and she smiled. "We ran a series on local heroes. Steven sent us information on you. We interviewed him for the story. Didn't he tell you?"

So that was how Kylie knew about his endeavors, not of her own accord. Nick's ego deflated a bit. He reclaimed the seat.

"No. Steven never mentioned it." Good thing his brother was already laid up, because Nick wanted to wring his neck.

He had enlisted in the military to do his part to protect his country. It wasn't personal. It was duty. Leaving a friend in the lurch and abandoning the woman he loved—that was personal. And he had failed on both accounts. Hardly a hero.

"The article received a lot of interest. Folks were quite impressed by the job you were doing to protect our country." Deeper color flooded Kylie's cheeks.

"Well, I suppose everyone could look good on paper. I'm a skilled soldier, nothing more. However," he added after a pause, "I appreciate the tribute."

Although a stretch, he didn't want to sound ungrateful, for Kylie's sake.

"Hero or not, I'm glad that you're keeping an eye on Kylie." Max stood and squeezed Kylie's shoulder before he walked away. "Keep me posted on any new developments."

"Sure, Max." Kylie shook her head.

The vibes Nick was getting from Kylie's editor were leaving him wary. "Is this guy for real?"

"If you mean, is he really only in it for the story? Then probably."

Nick locked eyes with Kylie and settled back in his seat. Absently, he scratched his jaw. "I believe we have our first suspect."

"What?" Kylie's mouth fell open. "Max is crazy, but not *crazy* crazy."

"Guilty, sweetheart, until proven otherwise."

"I believe it's the other way around."

"Not in my book."

# EIGHT

Over the next couple days, seconds ticked by like hours.

Bumping up her stride, Kylie paced the length of the living room to the kitchen and back again, pausing every now and again to glance out the window. Waiting was something she had never been good at, and with her stalker still on the loose, overcoming that flaw wasn't happening.

"Hey." Nick caught her by the hand, interrupting her next step. "Remember, stalkers try not to be obvious. So I doubt he plans to come strolling up the driveway."

Absently, Kylie whirled toward him. "I can't sit around and do nothing."

"Sure you can." Nick gestured to a seat at the table.

She hesitated, torn between her repetitious march and taking a break and sitting. A tangle of nerves knotted her stomach. Neither option enticed her.

A moment later, Nick pulled out the chair and twisted it slightly, the legs skidding against the hardwood floor. "Here. Now sit. You can see out the window." He patted the seat.

Great. He was making fun of her.

Not that she blamed him. If she were him, she'd

think she was crazy, too. Burning a path from one room to another, as if that would resolve anything.

Nick resumed his seat, leaned back in it and folded his arms across his chest.

Kylie drew in a breath, discounting the paranoid voice in her head. She hated feeling anxious. Then again, waiting for the next threat of terror wasn't easy.

Spent from restless sleep and frustrated, Kylie dropped onto the padded seat and blew out a breath. "Okay. I'm officially sitting around and doing nothing. Satisfied?"

"Oh, yes. Very." A tease in his voice.

Kylie shifted her gaze and found his familiar coffee-brown eyes staring back, glinting in amusement. Warmth curled through her, relaxing her shoulders and bumping up her heart rate. She couldn't help but smile at Nick's antics. His ability to spike her emotions with a glance still amazed her.

She gave herself a mental shake. She needed to keep a rein on her wayward emotions. Once the ordeal with her stalker was over and his brother healed, Nick would be out of her life again.

Once more tension grabbed at her muscles. Alarmed at how easily romantic notions took hold of her heart, she reined in every fanciful thought, vowing to stay focused.

"You need to relax." Nick leaned in, closing his large hand around her smaller one, giving her a reassuring squeeze. "Getting stressed out isn't going to help us solve this case."

Kylie pulled her hand away before melancholy thoughts could take over again. Straightening in her seat, she flexed her fingers, still warm from his touch. "But if the killer doesn't make contact with me soon, we'll never get this case solved."

Nick pushed back in his chair and drummed his long fingers on the wooden armrest. He looked way too relaxed for someone traipsing through the same nightmare she was. "Don't worry. He'll be in touch."

"Let's hope so."

"Remember, I've got your back," he said with a wink.

Hearing him say that brought tears to her eyes. She blinked to keep them at bay and sent up a silent prayer, asking for strength and a clear mind. She didn't want to put too much trust in this man. "Thank you. It's just hard to wait. Especially since I don't know what to expect next."

A glint of understanding entered his eyes. "It is hard to wait, and your stalker knows that."

Kylie hated being manipulated. Drawing a deep breath, she mumbled, "I wish he would call so we could just get this over with."

A hearty laugh deepened the indentions on either side of Nick's face. "And to think a few days ago you were worried that your phone might ring."

"So true." Kylie rubbed her hand along her

jeans, trying to flatten out a wrinkle beside the seam rather than look at Nick. Just a fleeting glance at his infamous smile and her willpower not to fall in love with him again was greatly in jeopardy.

"Funny how your priorities change when there's a target on your back." She worked up a pleasant smile. "After three days without a word from him, I'm getting a bit antsy."

"Remember, every move this guy makes is strategically planned. He wants you off guard. This is his ball game and he wants to remind us that he's in charge."

Kylie shrank back against the chair and crossed her arms. "Believe me, I'm quite aware. Frankly, this guy's boldness scares me to death. Not only is he watching every move I make, he broke into the house and made sure I heard him, while knowing you were only steps away."

Nick gave a slow nod and his eyes narrowed. "This is the worst kind of predator. Psychopaths like him thrive on thrill-seeking, risk-taking behavior. The riskier the chances, the more the endorphin rush. They purposely leave clues and become experts in concealing their identity. The more they get away with, the more powerful they feel."

"I hope that's not the good news."

Nick chuckled at that. "The guy thinks he's

invincible. He'll get sloppy, cut corners somewhere. That's when we'll catch him."

She glanced Nick's way. "And in the meantime?"

"Wait."

That was the part she didn't like.

A shiver danced up her spine and Kylie jumped to her feet. She needed to get moving again, burn off some anxiety. Huffing a sigh, she lengthened her stride toward the living room. Saturdays used to be fun. She wished now that she'd gone in to work.

"Okay. Time to go."

Kylie halted, whirled around to face Nick. "You're leaving me?"

"Nope. We're going on a walk." Nick grabbed their jackets off a peg by the door.

"But I thought you were compiling facts and clues in a flowchart format."

"I already finished. If you had stayed seated long enough, you would have noticed." He sent her another toe-curling smile.

*Brother.* Give him a couple days without drama and he was all smiles and charm. She swallowed, refocused. "So quickly. Any revelation?"

He hitched one muscular shoulder. "We need more facts."

"What are your thoughts so far?"

"You're not going to like them."

She wrinkled her nose. "Not Max again?"

Nick nodded. "Nothing conclusive, but he fits the mold. He knows your schedule, your personal information and has a vested interest in a big story."

"Max, a stalker?" Kylie thought out loud, trying to digest the notion. It wasn't happening. "He's a lot of things, but not that."

"Okay, consider this scenario." Nick squinted an eye and held up a finger. "The guy causes havoc in your life, then insists you write about it. He gets media coverage and also gets to watch his victim squirm. A serial killer's dream."

"You really believe Max orchestrated this so I can report his brutal crimes, all the way up until—" she had to force the words out "—the time he murders me?"

Nick instantly sobered. "Just a theory at the moment."

She appreciated Nick's expertise and hard work, but she would reserve speculating on Max for the time being. She breathed deep, thinking she should feel some relief from that. Then again, they had no other leads. Meaning anyone and everyone she knew was still a suspect.

Suddenly, she felt antsier than ever. She needed air. "What about that walk?"

Nick tossed her jacket to her.

A clear blue sky made a nice backdrop for the endless sea of evergreens and majestic mountains.

The air was crisp and refreshing. With all the banter about the killer's motives and such, Nick needed a breather as much as Kylie.

Nick rested against the porch railing and waited as Kylie zipped up her jacket. He caught the gleam of her silky dark curls, ruffled by the slight breeze. He couldn't imagine anything happening to her.

Something hard and tight lodged in Nick's chest. He breathed through it, allowing the fresh mountain air to calm him and get his mind back on track.

Nick refused to let fear creep in and distract him. He needed to stay calm for Kylie's sake. He was a soldier who knew how to put his emotions aside, do what was needed—a perspective he needed to keep in mind.

He glanced over at Kylie. "Steven told me about a trail about a quarter mile from here. It leads to a granite dome overlooking a valley. Great view, I hear."

Kylie's face brightened. "What are we waiting for?"

Nick took that as a yes. He fingered his waistband, making sure his phone was in place. "Okay, let's go."

They hiked up a small slope, the roar of waterfalls and birds in the distance. For the better part of an hour they threaded their way through bristly trees and tangled vegetation, then followed a narrower trail of sparser growth and knobby tree roots. As Kylie stayed close by his side, the forest around them evoked memories of better times, when he and Kylie had explored miles of Blue Ridge trails.

They had been young, so in love.

A familiar ache clutched his chest. Nick let out a slow breath, tried to recover.

There was nothing he could do to guard against the irrational feelings that came when he least expected. Ten years should have been enough time to move on from the past.

But one look at Kylie and he was eighteen again.

His life had spiraled out of control so quickly. One day he was a big man on campus, captain of the football team and boyfriend to the cutest girl in school. The next day, he was met by averted glances and shaking heads. He didn't blame his classmates. He should have been there for Conrad.

Rejection and loss had intensified the guilt and sadness that already saddled his shoulders. He hadn't been able to sleep or eat, or even be around Kylie.

Nothing in Asheville would ever be the same for him. So he'd given himself an ultimatum: stay cooped up in this little town where the shadows of the past would be ever present, or make a clean break and start fresh.

His choice shut Kylie out of his life.

Running away hadn't been easy, but coming back was worse.

The crest of the hill neared. He pushed all that aside as his focus changed. He stepped up his pace.

"Hey." Kylie's voice came from behind him.

Nick stopped midstride. He wheeled around. "Sorry, I didn't mean to get ahead of you."

Kylie grabbed onto a branch to help her up the embankment. Her soft-soled shoes slipped a bit. "Good. I thought maybe you were trying to ditch me."

He chuckled at that, hoping that wasn't really what she believed. "Never." He caught her hand, pulling her up to a level spot.

"Thank you." She leaned against a tree and caught her breath.

"You're welcome."

Her long lashes flicked up at him. "It's hard, isn't it?"

Nick studied her. "What's hard?"

She shrugged and walked toward him. "Being back in Ashville and being here with me." The look on her face was both tender and apologetic.

His pulse slowed. Had he been that obvious? "I'm sorry. I don't want you think I was ignoring you. I just—"

She shot up her hand. "No excuses. I understand."

Nick stared at her, feeling the fragile state of their relationship start to crumble. He'd never want her to think that he didn't care about her. "Kylie, you don't understand."

"Nick, I know that spending time with me, let alone protecting me from a raving lunatic, wasn't what you had in mind when you arrived in Asheville." She paused, her lips together for a moment. "And I realize how unfair it is that you got sucked into my problems."

True, his original plans hadn't included seeing Kylie, but now that their paths had connected, he wasn't going anywhere. "I have no intention of letting you walk through this alone."

A succinct answer, because the truth of his motives to get in and out of Asheville without stirring up the dust of the past was far more complicated.

"No, Nick." Kylie shoved back her hair. "You need to concentrate on keeping up Bentley's Hardware Store and helping your brother get back on his feet."

That wasn't even an option. He shook his head. "It's not that simple."

She kept a glare of insistence on her face, making him uneasy. "Simple or not, I don't want you involved in this as atonement for the past."

*So that's it.* Nick didn't like the way that sounded. Even if there was a thread of truth involved. "Kylie, I want you safe. Nothing more."

She started to speak, then fell silent, but her green eyes told him all he needed to know. She didn't believe him.

Finally she shrugged, her voice even. "I decided to put in for some vacation time and go visit my family for a while. Maybe it will throw the stalker off and put him back into hiding, or make him so mad that he'll make a fatal mistake that will lead to his arrest."

Nick huffed under his breath. "You know that's not likely. He's riled up and ready. No matter where you are, you're not safe."

Kylie's eyes misted over. "It's just too hard, Nick."

Waiting for the stalker to make his move? Or being with him? Either way, he understood.

"Kylie, listen." Nick reached a hand out toward her, then dropped it when she shuffled back a step.

"I'm serious." Her firm words defied the uncertainty in her voice.

He was serious, too. She wasn't leaving and he planned to stick by her side through this ordeal. And he would have told her so, had it not been for the manic bleating of her cell phone.

Kylie jerked, her eyes rounded. She plunged her hand into her coat pocket and retrieved her phone. She held it to her ear. "Hello."

Nick scratched his jaw and waited. Long moments passed like an eternity. Kylie didn't speak, didn't budge, until finally, she said, "Thank you, I'll be right over."

She clicked off the phone and took a deep breath.

"What's going on, Kylie?"

She blinked up at him, disbelief chasing across

her features. "That was Dave Michelson. They've found another body."

Nick narrowed his gaze. "And why do they think this body is related to our case?"

Kylie paused, swallowed. "His throat was slit."

# NINE

Kylie struggled to think. As a journalist, she'd reported on plenty of homicide cases. Careless, impulsive acts, usually the result of family disputes or drug-related crimes. But the senseless slayings over the past few days, coupled by a possible connection to Conrad's murder, took on a whole new dimension. This was out of her league—and her comfort zone.

Too bad she was stuck in the middle of it.

Yellow crime-scene tape marked a section of dense forest adjacent to the Black Hawk rest area. The crime scene, just two miles from her home, swirled with blue-and-red strobe lights, nervous energy, officers and dogs.

Kylie sighed and leaned against the front fender of a police cruiser. Hands shoved into her coat pockets, she refrained from checking her watch again. At last glance, two hours had passed and of that time ninety minutes had elapsed since Nick took off with Dave to investigate the area where the body was found.

This time she couldn't convince Dave to allow her into the crime scene. Thankfully, he'd enlisted Nick's help. His expertise gave her some comfort.

Kylie balled her fingers into fists in her pockets. Waiting for answers was brutal. She'd tried to relax, prayed, did a few stretches. Nothing helped.

She drew in a deep breath, the air muggy and heavy. Not quite the revival she hoped for. "God will prevail," she muttered under her breath. A trace of solace trickled through her.

To her right, a branch snapped, underbrush rustled. Dave poked past a dense section of trees and strode into the clearing, brushing dirt from his hands. A distant crackle of thunder punctuated what she feared was a precursor to more bad news.

She lifted her gaze. In spite of the storm looming in the distance, the sky above them remained an indigo-blue, with only a few wispy clouds. She felt a little better.

Two seconds later Nick emerged from the same path and headed toward her, following at Dave's heels.

"We scoured the area. Pretty clean. Nothing in the way of evidence." Dave removed his hat and swiped a bead of sweat from his forehead with the back of his thumb.

"How about footprints?" Kylie asked.

"A lot of fresh dirt was scattered around, but no definable shoe print. Looks like the victim was killed and then dumped here. No other signs of foul play."

"A dead body is enough foul play for me." Nick nodded at Dave, then looked at Kylie. He raised one eyebrow. "You okay?"

"I've had better days."

Nick smiled. "I'm right there with you, Ky."

*Ky.* He hadn't called her that in…forever. Her chest tightened and breathing became a whole new challenge. The logical side of her brain reminded her that life with Nick was over.

Too much time and history between them.

Too bad emotion trumped sensibility at the moment.

"Just remember, this guy's days are numbered. He may think he's brilliant, but we have a lot of brainpower on our side." Nick sidled up to her, and his comforting arm slipped around her shoulder. This time she didn't pull away.

His optimism comforted her almost as much as his presence. Kylie wanted nothing more than to melt into his arms and erase the past ten years of their lives. Start anew.

No more unsolved murders. No more guilt.

Of course, that scenario wasn't going to happen. Her irrational thoughts brought tears to her eyes, sparked her anger and made her heart ache all at the same time, reminding her of how much she'd lost.

And worse, the nightmare that had started ten years ago still continued.

Fighting a sigh, she raised two fingers to her throbbing temple, rotating them in gentle circles.

This man standing beside her definitely had the power to break her heart again.

What she needed was a little space from him. Or better yet, a whole new life, complete with a husband, a couple kids and a dog or cat, maybe even a gerbil. After this mess was over, that would be her goal. Find a nice guy, settle down. Maybe Florida would be a good place to—

"About the last phone call, Kylie."

Dave's voice broke up her rambling thoughts. He shifted his weight from one foot to the other, looking tired. Apparently, this case was wearing on him, too.

"Although we have your cell tapped, there was a lot of static on our end. So, let's go over what the caller said. Did he mention anything about another murder?" Dave continued, "Even a remote hint from him could help us."

Kylie shook off the chills racing through her extremities as she thought over Dave's question. Even as each word of the dreadful conversation replayed in her head, nothing stood out as a hint. "Sorry, Dave. The caller didn't insinuate anything about another murder. How long do you think the victim has been out here?"

Dave gave a shrug. "Not too long. Three, maybe four hours tops. Rigor mortis hadn't set in yet. Blood was still oozing from the wound when he was found."

*Great.* Kylie swallowed against a dry throat. More detail than she cared to know. "The person who found him didn't see anything?"

"No." Dave shook his head. "It was a man and his wife. They spotted the body when they walked to the picnic tables to have lunch. There were no other vehicles in the area. They probably just missed the culprit."

"So you both agree that this crime is related to the airport murder and most likely Conrad's?" She looked at Dave and then Nick.

Dave gave a single nod and Nick's frown deepened the creases around his eyes and answered her question even before he replied, "Afraid so."

As much as she was inclined to agree, she still held an inkling of hope that this was an unrelated murder. She hated to believe that the man who was stalking her was on a killing rampage.

"Too many similarities." Dave fixed his smoky gaze on her as if he could read her mind. "One precision slash across the neck. No other injuries noted, like the last victim and Conrad."

Kylie's pulse quickened and she shoved the images of the other victims from her mind, afraid of what her churning stomach might do if she allowed them to surface.

"Detective Michelson, look at this." A voice rose above the commotion around them.

Dave turned on the heel of his boot as a police officer, short and thick, with a harried expression on his face, hustled toward the detective. "One of the dogs uncovered this." He held up a wallet tangled in slimy moss.

Dave dug a pair of gloves from his pocket and pulled them on. "Can't beat those canine noses." He took it from the officer, peeled away the green bog, then opened it and went through the contents.

"This guy's getting bolder all the time and not as careful." Nick brushed up closer to her, tightening his hold around her shoulders. A warm charge zipped up her spine. Of course, Nick was merely attempting to calm her, although it was completely backfiring.

"He's pushing his limits, ditching a body in a rest area off the parkway in broad daylight," Nick said, then added, "It is just a matter of time."

"Sooner rather than later, I hope." Kylie eased away from him, out of the warmth of his embrace, hoping to clear her thoughts and create a safer distance between them.

Crossing her arms, she eyed Nick, waiting for him to elaborate about the crime scene. He wasn't looking at her, though. His attention was on Dave as he went through the wallet.

For the first time since they'd left the mountain, Kylie studied Nick. Mud caked the soles of his scuffed boots and the green camo jacket over his white polo also bore splotches of dirt. He had a placid look on his face and his dark gaze seemed to haze over, revealing concern.

Kylie's insides twisted into a tight knot. She was appalled at how irritable and insensitive she'd been earlier. He wasn't to blame for this nightmare or the fact that her heart still clung to the past. He'd moved on and owed her nothing. Yet he continued to walk through this trial with her, helping her stay safe and strong. A man of noble character. If nothing else, he was a good friend.

That would have to be enough. Before she had time to fully convince herself of that fact, she heard Dave mutter, "Well, I'll be."

Kylie whirled toward him. "What is it?"

Dave waved a small card. "The victim's ID. Thomas Crosby, from Hampton, Virginia. Have you ever heard of him?"

Kylie took the laminated card and studied the picture on the front. "He doesn't look familiar." She handed it back to Dave.

Dave's gaze moved from the card in his hand to Kylie and back again. After a seeming eternity, he cleared his throat. "Well, if you don't know Mr. Crosby, the killer may have planted this, too."

"Planted what?" She was almost afraid to ask.

Dave tugged a small photo from the wallet's plastic sleeve.

Squinting at the picture, it took a moment before Kylie recognized her own high-school graduation photo.

Kylie stared, dismayed, as her blood turned to ice, sending an unwelcome shiver dancing up her spine. "Why is this happening?"

Nick shook his head. "Don't let this get to you. Think of it as the predator's calling card. He's letting us know he was responsible. One more clue. That's what you need to remember." His voice was low, but firm.

Tears of disbelief nearly blinded Kylie. Stunned, she nodded.

Logically, that statement sounded reasonable. Emotionally, nothing did.

Late that same evening, Nick sat at his brother's kitchen table, his hand cupped around a mug of coffee. As he looked over the updated flowchart on the table in front of him, a menacing ache filled his chest. He still had no conclusive evidence.

Serial killers were smart, crafty and patient, so the lack of clues shouldn't surprise him. He set down his nearly empty mug and lifted a hand to massage his left temple. There had to be something he was missing. And that something was driving him crazy.

So far the only fact he was certain of was that there was a maniac out there who had access to Kylie.

Chills marched down the length of his arms as that thought rooted in his mind. It had to be someone she knew. One of their high-school classmates could be the culprit. Or even a friend from church, a coworker or a neighbor. Then again, there was her editor.

Nick applied more pressure to his temple, rubbing vigorously. *Or the man in the moon.*

He bumped a fist against the table. Facts. He needed facts. Something to zero in on. He hated maybes and at the moment, that was all he had. He shoved back from the table and rose. The back of his chair smacked into the wall.

"Still nothing?"

The softness of Kylie's voice had its usual calming effect on him and the evening suddenly got brighter.

Nick swung his head to the doorway and stared at her, bundled in her chenille robe, the hem of silky pajama pants brushing against her ankles. She had scrubbed her face clean, wet curls framing her face. He drew a deep breath, feeling strangely rejuvenated at her relaxed demeanor and simple beauty. She was a sight to behold.

"Slow progress." He worked up a small grin.

When her lips parted into a smile, his heart warmed a little more.

Rising, he strode toward her. "With all the chaos since I've been here, I haven't had a chance to tell you how beautiful you still look."

Kylie shook her head, tugged the sash on her robe. "Oh, Captain Bentley, you are definitely sleep deprived."

"Nope. I noticed the moment I saw you. You haven't changed at all."

The twitch of humor at the corners of Kylie's lips slowly turned into a full-fledged grin. "Well, outside of a few extra pounds, maybe."

*In all the right places.* Nick caught himself before that comment slipped out.

"Actually, you look pretty good yourself." Kylie braced one shoulder against the archway wall and crossed her arms. The collar of her pink robe inched up, nestling lightly at the base of her neck and complimenting the cherry flush on her cheeks. "Although I'd hoped that by now you might be touting a nice burly paunch. Or at least have a few wiry hairs protruding from your ears or nostrils."

He laughed, completely understanding. A big wart on her nose might have been just the thing to keep his haywire emotions on track. But then again…probably not. He cleared his throat and refocused. "Sorry to disappoint you. Give me a couple decades, and my midsection and extraneous whiskers should be thriving."

Laughter gleamed in her crystal-green eyes. That was another thing about Kylie he remembered, the way her whole face lit up when she relaxed. Genuine pleasure. Her eyes twinkled first, and then her smile turned lethal.

His heartbeat kicked up in response. He tore his gaze away from her face with more effort than he cared to admit. No other woman had affected him like that.

Dangerous soil, that was what he was treading on.

Seeing her finally unwind catapulted him back

to their high-school years. A time of youth and love and dreams of a future together. When they had both believed that nothing could tear them apart. But Nick had learned the hard way that life could change at a moment's notice, altering every plan and every direction.

"About this morning, Nick." Kylie's smile faded and her expression turned somber. "I said some things that probably sounded unappreciative. Please don't think that I am. I do appreciate your help. I just don't want to be a burden to you."

"A burden?" Nick shook his head and moved a step closer. "Don't ever think that. We're in this together."

Color drained from her face. For a moment, she simply stood there and said nothing. Finally, she mumbled, "In it together? Like the night Conrad died?"

*Conrad?* "I don't understand what you're getting at."

Her gaze clung to his. She caught her bottom lip with her teeth. "Never mind. It doesn't matter."

It did matter. The wary look in her eyes told him that. Just seeing that distress dredged up old feelings that he'd buried deep in the furthest reaches of his being. Conrad's death had left a mark on so many, but the pain flaring in Kylie's gaze belonged to Nick.

"What is it, Kylie?"

She said nothing, simply stood there with a troubled cast to her delicate features.

Then it hit him. "Do you think I blame you?" He narrowed his eyes and pointed a thumb back at his chest.

"You should," she answered in a matter-of-fact way. "I wheedled you into sneaking out of camp that night."

One step more and Nick stood toe-to-toe with her. So close he could see specks of gold in her eyes and the little tremor in her lip. He wanted to kiss her. He really did. Fortunately, good sense prevailed. "Kylie, I never blamed you and still don't."

She gave him a doleful look. "You had second thoughts about hiking to the overlook. Because of my selfishness you went against your instincts and came with me."

Nick's heart twisted at the misperception. "Kylie, I learned a long time ago that a man makes his own decisions."

"However, sometimes those decisions are made out of duty." She lifted her lashes and glared at him.

He frowned, not liking the direction of her thoughts. He already carried enough guilt for the both of them. "I made the choice, Kylie. My choice. My responsibility."

"Very noble, Captain." She hiked up her chin.

"However, that nobility turned into a curse. You took claim to a burden that didn't belong to you."

Nick scratched his head. "That's a bit overstated."

Kylie met his eyes, the intensity in her gaze unmistakable. "Nick. You didn't kill Conrad. After years of beating myself up with shame, I finally came to grips with the fact that my childish antics didn't put Conrad in his grave. By God's grace, my guilt was lifted and I'm desperately trying to move on."

"I'm happy for you. No point in staying locked in the past."

There was a heartbeat of hesitation before she responded, "When are you going to let go of the past, Nick?"

He swallowed, feeling as if a clenching fist had hold of his larynx. She didn't understand. Couldn't understand.

Hurt flashed briefly in Kylie's emerald eyes before he saw the sheen of unshed tears. "You blame yourself. You blame God. Maybe I should spend the rest of my life accepting the blame."

A beat passed and before he could respond, she shot up her hand. "No, wait. You've got guilt covered. And that's the part I hate." She swallowed, glanced away.

He hated that, too. Gently, he caught her chin with his fingers and turned her face to look at him. "I think we're getting off track. There's a killer on the loose, a stalker. That in itself evokes a lot of emotions. Let's put what happened ten years ago behind us and concentrate on today."

Kylie blinked, and then nodded. "You're probably right. But I hope you'll make use of your own advice about not holding on to the past."

"I'm working on it." Nick dredged up a smile. As he caught her gaze again, he saw a glimmer of hope in her eyes. Her confidence inspired him, but that didn't make letting go of the past any easier.

# TEN

The very next morning, around eleven o'clock, Kylie had high hopes of a nice peaceful brunch with Nick. But instead, as they sat on a lobby bench and waited for a table at the Egg Masters Café on Main Street, she mentally counted the curious glances from across the room. Nick didn't seem to notice. He had his nose stuck in a menu.

She glanced at her watch. Twenty-two minutes and counting. Keeping her eyes averted, she picked up a menu and started to peruse the list of options, although she already knew what she wanted to order. Still, she allowed her gaze to rove the laminated pages, trying not to let the spectators distract her.

Fear and tension had quickened the pulse of this once-quiet city. The recent homicides were big news and had become a hot topic for residents, especially with the possible link to Conrad's unsolved murder. Since Kylie continued to cover the story, not to mention being the killer's contact person, her friends and neighbors considered her a key informant. If she even dared to cast a glance at one of the familiar faces, it would be an open invitation for them to start asking questions. Something she'd learned the hard way over the years.

This was the part of her job that frustrated her most. People assumed she knew more than she reported. Which, in this case, wasn't correct.

Outside of investigating her graduating class, the case had added up to zilch. And they'd yet to come up with a possible connection between victims. The investigators and forensic team were working furiously, although still lacking crucial details.

Kylie shifted uncomfortably against the hard bench. She couldn't help wondering if one of those curious glances belonged to her stalker.

That thought tightened her gut and sent shivers along the fine hairs at the base of her neck. More than anyone, she understood the danger of this killer.

Pushing aside her turbulent thoughts, she glanced at Nick, still totally engrossed in breakfast options.

"Did you find anything you might like?"

Nick lowered his menu enough for her to glimpse his dark chocolate eyes. "Are you kidding? I'm trying to narrow it down. It's been years since I've seen this many choices for breakfast."

Kylie slapped a hand to her chest, feigning surprise. "What? The military didn't offer thirty-two varieties of omelets to their soldiers?"

With a chuckle, Nick pressed his elbow into hers. "Do you think I would have left if they had?"

Was that all it took to keep him around? A

vast breakfast menu? She bit her lower lip, fighting down a sigh, wishing he would stick around. Wishing he had a reason to stay.

Nick tucked the menu into the metal holder on the wall, then thumped back against the bench and folded his arms. "Actually, my team and I got excited at the sight of a hard-boiled egg. Our tours didn't afford much in the way of family diners."

"Well, then, I guess it's good to be home." She slanted a glance at him, crossed her fingers and said a prayer.

The glint in Nick's eyes faded and his lips drew into a fine line before he gave a shrug. "It's good for now."

That was what she was afraid of. Her heart sank a little.

"Bentley. Party of two." The waitress appeared from around the corner. She grabbed two packages of silverware from a tub beside the register and gestured for them to follow.

There was nothing fancy about this place. The waitstaff wore blue jeans and T-shirts and the decor ranged from an eclectic collection of weathered farm tables and mismatched wooden chairs to a colorful array of antique paintings on the walls.

Homey and cozy. She liked that. And having Nick here with her, well…nostalgic thoughts came rushing back. This had been a favorite eatery of theirs. Affordable and good food. A nice combination for high-school students with minimal funds.

The waitress seated them at a small table in the corner. Kylie sank onto the chair by the wall and noticed Nick's quick scan of the patrons before he took the seat across from her. The same encompassing glance that he gave when they walked in. He never left his training behind. How could she not feel safe with this man?

Amid her mixed feeling about having him around, she figured God knew what He was doing.

The day was shaping up to be good. The pastor's message about trust and belief had inspired her and Nick had actually managed to stay awake through it all. Maybe the army had softened him some. Maybe someday he'd believe again—

*Stop it!* Suppressing a sigh, she unraveled her napkin and placed silverware on either side of her woven place mat.

Nick leaned forward, planted his forearms on the table. "What are you having?"

She smoothed the napkin across her lap. "Spinach omelet and whole-wheat toast."

He angled his head, his brow crinkling. "Just spinach? A little boring, isn't it?"

She shrugged. "A healthy choice and delicious."

Then came the chuckle. "Thirty-two varieties of omelets and you want spinach?"

It still took her breath away to witness the gleam of delight in his eyes when he laughed. "I know what I like."

Nick picked up a menu, glancing at it again. "I

guess that would make ordering easier. I'm trying to decide between the jalapeno-and-taco-meat omelet and the mighty meat lover's."

"Difficult choices." She smiled, but her churning abdomen couldn't afford any surprises. "I'm in the mood for something familiar and predictable."

"Familiar and predictable?" Lowering his menu, he raised an eyebrow. "Like Asheville?"

"Yeah. Although lately—" she looped a stray lock of hair behind her ear "—not so predictable."

"Hopefully, that will change soon."

"Let's hope so." She nodded and then asked, "What about you?"

"Me? I don't know." He gave a small yawn and leaned back in his seat. "It's been years since familiar and predictable have been part of my vocabulary. I'm not sure what I like anymore."

Kylie fought off another sigh. She knew exactly what she liked and she was staring at him right now.

When breakfast was about over, Nick motioned to the waitress. "Could we have refills on our drinks, please?"

Balancing plates in her hands, she nodded. "Someone will be there in a moment."

"Did you enjoy your meal?" Kylie really didn't have to ask as Nick shoveled the last of his omelet into his mouth.

He swallowed his bite. "A meat-lover's omelet and buttermilk biscuits. What could be better?"

"Spinach and wheat toast." She tilted her head and met his eyes, egging him on and enjoying the grin that erupted across his jaw.

"You guys need refills?" With a coffee carafe in one hand and a pitcher of water in the other, the hostess, Lindsay Potter, stopped at their table.

Before Kylie or Nick could answer the question, the woman's jaw dropped. "Nick Bentley?"

Glancing up, he said, "Guilty as charged." Although not looking too guilty.

"It seems like forever since I've seen you. Do you remember me?"

Nick gave a tight grin. "Lindsay Potter, right?"

Lindsay nodded, her eyes all for Nick. "I was just thinking about you when I heard about your brother's accident. I wondered if you'd be coming around." She took a step closer and slid a pitcher on the table.

Nick gave a lazy shrug. "I'll be around to help out for a while."

"That's awesome. We've missed you around here." Lindsay beamed, fingering a lock of her blond hair, piled high, ringlets spilling down. She was still attractive and voluptuous. Her figure-hugging jeans attested to that, accentuating her long legs and every curve.

"Thanks. It's always good to be missed."

If missing him was good, Kylie won the prize. Absently, she smoothed hair from her face, wondering what it would be like to be blonde. Lindsay had been prom queen, head cheerleader and the most popular girl in school. Intimidating then... and now.

"Nick, I gotta tell you," Lindsay went on with a flirty giggle. "You really look great."

*Brother*. Kylie sank against the wooden back of her chair and turned her gaze to the scenery out the window.

"It looks as though you're doing well yourself," Nick responded.

Another giggle from Lindsay. "Thanks. I'm doing just fine, even better now that you're here. While you're in town, let's plan to get together sometime."

Kylie whipped her gaze back. Lindsay wasn't really asking him out?

The look of anticipation on Lindsay's face told her different. And with Kylie right there—Nick's old girlfriend. Some nerve. Even in high school Lindsay had hit on him a few times, and for all Lindsay knew, she and Nick could be dating again.

Kylie swallowed. But that wasn't the case.

A pause, then a shrug from Nick. "I don't know, Lindsay. I'm pretty busy."

Was he even considering it? Kylie fought not to cringe. Of course he was. He was male, after all. He hadn't died when their relationship fizzled. He'd probably had a list of romances since then. Kylie being the least of them.

"Come on, Nick. Surely you have a night or two free." Lindsay gracefully shifted her weight.

If she moved any closer to Nick, Kylie would just—do what? Nick was a friend, nothing more. He could see whom he wanted. Do what he wanted.

Dragging her gaze away, Kylie wadded up her napkin and dropped it on her plate. Jealousy wasn't usually an issue for her, but the heat swarming through her body certainly showed that wasn't the case now.

Breathing deep, Kylie waited a moment, then picked up her glass. It might be a good time for a little distraction before Lindsay tucked her phone number into Nick's hand. "Excuse me, Lindsay. Could I please have some more water?"

With a small huff, Lindsay snagged the decanter of water off the table and pivoted toward Kylie. "Here you go." She hastily tilted the pitcher, her movements so jerky she overfilled the glass, pouring water down Kylie's arm to her elbow, saturating her sleeve.

The icy-cold liquid made Kylie gasp. She let go of the glass, sending it crashing onto the table. Rivulets of water flowed in every direction, cascading over the table edge and onto her lap.

Jumping up, Kylie grabbed a napkin and began blotting her skirt, now sticking wetly to her legs. Molten heat crept into her cheeks.

Nick surged up from his seat, offering Kylie his

napkin, while Lindsay, still armed with two vessels of liquid, charged toward her.

"What can I do to help?"

"Nothing." Kylie shot up one hand while tugging down her skirt with the other.

"How about something else to drink, or maybe dessert? It will be on the house," Lindsay offered, gesturing with one of the carafes toward the kitchen.

"No. I'm good." Shivering, Kylie shook her head. "I just need to get to the ladies' room and dry off."

Equally embarrassed and annoyed, mostly at herself, Kylie snaked her way through the crowded section of tables. More curious glances, but this time for a very different reason.

Inside the bathroom, she pulled out several paper towels and blotted her skirt. Then she peeled off her sweater, wringing out the sleeve as she smirked at the rosy blush on her cheeks in the mirror. She should be embarrassed at the obvious way she'd interrupted Lindsay to put a stop to her flirtatious propositions.

So high-schoolish. Nick probably thought she was crazy.

Even in her sense of chagrin, Kylie had to laugh as she replayed the scene in her head.

She punched the metal button on the hand dryer mounted on the wall. Hot air spewed out. She held the sleeve of her sweater under it.

Next time she'd mind her own business.

*Lord, forgive me.*

A trill of her cell phone cut through the hum of the dryer and made her heart skip a beat. Dropping her sweater, she fished the handset out of her skirt pocket.

Swallowing, she held it to her ear. "Hello."

"Kylie." The deep, breathy drawl strained through the phone line.

Air evacuated her lungs. "Um…yes," she muttered, barely audible.

"Kylie. My precious Kylie. You sound upset."

"No, I'm—" Her voice broke. She pulled the receiver from her ear, cleared her throat and came back to the line. "I'm fine. Just tired."

"Oh, I'm glad to hear you're feeling well. I've missed talking to you. Have you missed me?"

Frustration welled in her chest. She hated playing games. "Please don't taunt me. I don't even know who you are."

"Oh, but you do."

A shudder ripped up Kylie's spine. She breathed deep, worked to keep her voice steady. "That's a pretty vague statement. Why don't you at least give me a hint?"

His raspy chuckle seeped through the line, raising the hairs on her neck. "It's not time for that yet, dear. I still have work to do."

A bubble of panic replaced the frustration in

her chest. She swallowed, pushing past the fear. "Work? What kind of work?"

A pause stretched across the phone line.

Kylie gritted her teeth. This conversation was ludicrous. He was baiting her. She took another deep breath. Made a decision to dig in, find out what she could. "Are you responsible for the murder at Black Hawk rest area?"

Silence. Longer this time.

Finally, he said, "Oh, Kylie, I'm flattered that you recognized my talent."

"Talent? You mean slaughter."

"Tsk, tsk, my dear. Cleaning the streets of the unlovely isn't slaughter."

"What?"

"Outcasts. Criminals. Predators on society."

*Like you.* Kylie bit her tongue. Desperate questions bubbled inside her mind. She snatched the most disturbing thought. "Is that what you thought Conrad was? An outcast or predator?"

Another period of silence lapsed. She waited. Second thoughts about her assumption that this man was involved in Conrad's death crossed her mind.

The man's heavy sigh shattered the hush. "A casualty, my dear. Conrad got in the way."

Got in the way of what? She tried to move her lips to shout the question. Tears flooded her eyes. This man had killed Conrad.

A heartbeat passed. Maybe two.

"Sweet Kylie, I'll be in touch."

"Wait—" she managed just before he hung up.

This time Nick was the one doing the pacing. By the white shaft of light illuminating them, Kylie watched him pace the length of Steven's living-room rug, hands jammed in his pockets. His ability to stay patient and calm had started to wane. Not a good thing. His strength helped keep her strong.

*Lord, help us both.*

"Are you sure the caller didn't imply anything about his next move? Or allude to what kind of work he had to do?"

Kylie settled back against the sofa and took a breath. "No. I guess I threw him off when I asked him about Conrad."

Nick stopped his march and shook his head, his eyes tunneling into hers. "Kylie, it's important that when this guy calls, you let him do the talking. We can deal with his twisted history later. We need to know what he's thinking now. Hopefully, he'll drop one too many clues that will lead us to him. And the longer he stays on the line, the better opportunity we have to trace him."

"Sorry." She shrugged. Of course, Nick was right. Impulsiveness had gotten her into trouble more than once.

"I know it's difficult to talk to the guy. But if you feel like you need to ask questions to keep the conversation going, focus on his future plans." Nick settled his hands on his hips and cocked his left knee. A stance from his football days. Only now instead of a teenage athlete, she was looking at a man. A soldier. Stronger. More powerful.

Kylie swallowed. "You're beginning to sound like Max."

Nick crossed his arms, one eyebrow hooked upward. "Maybe I underestimated the man."

"Really? What changed?"

"He's a journalist at heart. Maybe he is just looking for a story. Although his motives are skewed."

To say the least. "So he's off your suspect list for now?"

A crooked smile stretched across his lips. "Nope. He'll be on it until the case is solved."

"How often do your suspicions pay off?"

"I'm still alive, aren't I?"

She straightened her back and returned his smile. "Yes, you are." Very much so. And the intense way he was looking at her now would likely be the death of her.

She cleared her throat, pulled her mind back on track. "And what happens when this case is solved?"

"What do you mean?" Nick stared down at her, the smooth lines on his brow pleated.

"Well." She swallowed the rising lump in her throat and continued, "The other day you mentioned that Steven's recovery was going better than expected. If he's able to get back to work by the time this murder case is solved, will you be leaving?"

Leaning against the column in the living room, Nick crossed one ankle over the other and nodded his head. "Yeah, that's the plan. But honestly, I haven't been much help to Steven yet. I might hang around awhile and make sure he doesn't need anything. Then after I tie up a few loose ends, I'll figure out where to head next."

His quick acknowledgment knocked her off-balance. Not that she expected he'd changed his mind about leaving. She narrowed an eye on him. "Those loose ends wouldn't by chance involve Lindsay?"

Nick flashed her a baffled look. "Lindsay?"

Heat swarmed Kylie's cheeks, but she kept her chin up. "Lindsay Potter."

His dark eyebrows lifted. "What would make you think that?"

Kylie thought furiously, trying to figure out the best way to answer him without sounding like a meddling ex-girlfriend. It took only a moment before she realized there wasn't one. Or a good reason she'd asked the question in the first place.

Impulsivity. Would she ever learn? "Well, I thought you and Lindsay developed a nice rapport today."

Nick spurted out a booming laugh.

Okay. Maybe she was wrong.

"Actually, I was grateful when you finally interrupted her."

"Oh."

Straightening and fastening his hands more firmly on his hips, Nick looked at Kylie with such an amused grin that she couldn't help but grin back at him. "So you really thought I'd be interested in a woman like Lindsay?"

She shrugged. "She's cute and she's friendly."

"Come on, Kylie. You know me better than that. I've never been one for forward and flashy women."

He was assuming a lot. After ten years of no contact, how could she know who or what he liked these days? She probably was better off not knowing.

Another shrug. "Sorry. Just checking."

He sent her another killer grin and her heart slipped again. "Thanks for looking out for me."

"No problem." Not her entire motive, but at least she'd sleep a little easier tonight.

# ELEVEN

For the first time since Nick had arrived back in Asheville, the dread that had taken root in his gut had started to subside. He'd even had second thoughts about having breakfast with Kylie that morning at one of their old haunts, but that had turned out to be more enjoyable than stressful.

Pleasant memories were slowly trickling back to life, even with ongoing thoughts of Conrad's murder in the forefront of his mind. Something he hadn't considered possible.

Now, if he could just do something about Kylie's stalker.

With a sigh, Nick shifted his six-foot-two frame, stretching out on the couch in Steven's living room, trying to find a more comfortable position. An exercise in futility, he decided. Sofas weren't designed for someone his size. That was what beds were made for. Something he wasn't going to see tonight. He punched his pillow, curled it into a ball and shoved it back under his head.

Though he shouldn't complain—over the years he'd bunked in far worse accommodations.

With all the happenings over the past few days, he needed to be close to Kylie. And staying next door wasn't an option. Even his brother's room, on the opposite side of the house from where Kylie was sleeping, seemed too far away. Especially if she needed him. He could only imagine what the brazen stalker had in mind next.

Clearing his thoughts before his overactive imagination robbed his sleep, Nick rolled to his side and tugged up his bedsheet.

Hours later, he woke to the savory scent of bacon and coffee. With some effort, he sat up and swung his feet onto the floor. Morning light filtered in through the partially cracked window blinds. Squinting, he shielded his eyes and inhaled, pulling in the mouthwatering scent. Now fully awake, he smiled, thankful he wasn't imagining it.

He stood to arch his back, tight after his cramped sleeping position on the couch. After giving his limbs a good stretch, he dressed quickly and walked to the kitchen.

And there Kylie was. Busy at the stove, her back to him.

Hovering at the doorway, Nick took his time and studied her. Sunlight spilled in through the small window over the sink, accentuating the red and gold highlights in her hair. She wore a fitted denim dress with a dish towel tied around her waist as a makeshift apron and a pair of fuzzy slippers on her feet. An odd clothing combo, but Kylie Harper could pull it off.

Still a beauty, in every sense of the word.

"Good morning," he said finally.

Kylie spun to face him, a spatula in her hand. Her eyes widened as she audibly exhaled. "Nick, don't sneak up on me like that."

He shot his arms up in mock surrender. "Sorry. Blame it on the army. They trained us to walk silently. This gait took me years to perfect. Now I guess it's just second nature."

She gave him an appreciative grin. "When there's an enemy around, I suppose it's a good thing."

He returned the smile and lowered his hands. "It has come in handy a time or two. But if you'd like, I could give a whistle or maybe a yodel as a warning next time."

"I prefer a nice drumroll, but do what you can." She blinked up at him, a teasing gleam in her eyes.

He lifted a brow. "By the way, I don't think that spatula of yours would do much in the way of intimidation."

Kylie glanced at the plastic utensil in her hand. "I don't know. I have a pretty wicked tennis swing." Biting her lip, she gave a little demonstration.

Laughter rumbled deep in his chest as he settled into a chair at the table. "I think some pepper spray might be in order. I'll pick some up today."

"You may be right." Kylie turned back to the stove. "I hope Steven doesn't mind, but I found some bacon and eggs and sourdough bread. I decided to make breakfast. Do you still like French toast?"

Was she kidding? "Still one of my favorites. But don't tell me you're willing to stray from your infamous spinach omelet and wheat toast?"

"I'm more flexible at home." She glanced over her shoulder and smiled.

*At home—with Kylie.* Interesting concept, a fleeting thought that quickly abated. He didn't have a home anymore. With his vagabond past, he doubted he'd ever find a place to call home again.

"Kylie, what can I do to help you?"

"Nothing. Just sit there. You've helped me so much, this is the least I can do."

He did as she asked, enjoying the view, probably a little more than he should. Although he hadn't been much help yet. There was still a crazy man on the loose. An issue he planned to rectify soon.

Short minutes later, Kylie set a plate of food in front of him and took the seat across from his. Bowing her head, she said a short prayer. "Lord, bless this food to our bodies and protect us through the day."

Nick shifted in his seat. She really was serious about this faith thing.

Kylie blew out a long breath and pushed back a stray lock of hair. "I'm so glad Monday is here.

I usually love the weekend, but this one has been horrendous." She forked a bite of food.

Nick paused between bites. He raised one eyebrow. "Spending the weekend with me was that bad, huh?"

"No. I didn't mean that." Kylie lowered her fork and laughed. "What I meant to say was that this weekend has been a little too eventful for me. You know, crazy phone calls, dead bodies."

"Oh, that." Nick winked. "Glad it wasn't me."

Kylie dropped her gaze and forked another bite of food.

Great. He'd offended her. That was a pretty fresh move for someone she called a friend. His heart gave a thump, this time reminding him he needed to keep his head on straight. Kylie needed his help. Plain and simple. She didn't need him. Didn't want him.

He didn't blame her.

Payroll. Nick had never thought simple accounting could be so confusing. Swiveling in his office chair, he picked up a handful of time sheets and entered them into the first ledger. This was the same archaic system his father had used when Nick was an adolescent. Even then it had seemed redundant.

Everything was recorded on paper, transcribed into three ledgers before adding the total hours worked by each employee on the payroll record log. No wonder Steven said he stayed most of the night when he did payroll.

Blowing out a breath, Nick scribbled in some more numbers before realizing he had written them in the wrong column. Sighing, he grabbed an eraser.

Give him a laptop and he could figure out anything. Manual accounting was definitely over his head.

The next time Nick glanced up, his gaze shifted automatically to the large wall clock. Five-fifty. Great. He grabbed his cell phone and punched in Kylie's number. He was supposed to meet her at the newspaper office by six. The motorcycle had a flat tire this morning, so he'd dropped her off and still had her car.

He hated being late for anything. Especially for her.

Kylie picked up on the third ring. "Hey, Nick."

"Sorry, running late. It's payroll day and I'm struggling to relearn how to use a basic calculator. I'm leaving now and should be there in about fifteen minutes."

"Sounds stressful." He heard amusement in her voice. "Just take your time. I have a couple things to catch up on."

"Busy day for you, too?"

"Actually, there hasn't been much in the way of breaking news. Which has been kind of nice. I need a slow day once in a while. Most of the other reporters have left for the day, so I haven't had any distractions."

Alone? Nick didn't like that idea. "Anyone there with you?"

"Ray and Don, a couple of guys in the print department, are working just down the hall. But no one gets into the building without a code or a key after security leaves at five."

Nick scratched his temple. *Except criminals.* He spared her that thought. "I'm glad you're not alone. I'll be on my way shortly. I'll call when I get there."

"I'll be ready."

Kylie settled back in her seat and scrolled through files on her computer. She stopped halfway through the list and opened one. *Local 4-H club and their farm animals get ready to compete at state fair.* Nibbling her lip, she skimmed over the first draft of the article.

It was a good start. Satisfied, she picked up a yellow legal pad and tore off a page of notes. She ran her finger down the page, rechecking the breed of sheep the students would be showing at the fair.

*Suffolk.* That was what she'd thought.

She turned back to the computer and started typing.

The sound of heavy footsteps striking the tile floor drifted in from the hallway. She stopped, sat up straighter in her chair. She glanced around, expecting to see one of her colleagues walk into the newsroom.

Several moments passed. Nothing. She shook her head. She hated when her mind conjured up fears.

Kylie picked up typing again.

A soft ruffling sound came from behind her and she tensed. Whirling in her seat, she shot a sharp glance to the doorway. She waited and then shouted, "Hello. Ray? Don?"

No answer. That didn't stop the dread knotting in her stomach.

She picked up the phone and dialed the print-shop extension. Seven rings later she hung up. They must have gone to dinner.

Okay. Enough work for one day. She'd just wait outside for Nick. Stuffing her cell phone into her pocket, she hitched her handbag onto her shoulder.

Another sound drifted toward her. Soft foot-falls?

Her breath caught in her lungs. She wasn't waiting to find out. She headed for the back exit off the anteroom that led to the lower parking lot, chiding herself for being skittish.

Then again, whoever was milling around could have at least made themselves known.

Even the janitor poked his head in and said hello before he started working. Circling the copy machine, she swung past several reels of newsprint and boxes of ink. As she approached a wall of employee lockers, she heard her name. She paused to listen; the drone of the air conditioner filled the silence. But as she took her next step, the thud of boots made her pulse surge.

In three quick steps, she reached the exit door and yanked it open. Anxiously, she ran her hand along the stairwell wall, searching for the light switch. She scarcely used this exit and couldn't recall the location.

Something hard and metallic clunked on the floor. Abandoning her search, she moved quickly, groping her way down the narrow staircase, stumbling twice before she reached the first-floor landing.

As she took a moment to catch her breath, a door slammed and she heard footsteps thundering down behind her.

Panic zipped along her spine, sending her into fight-or-flight mode. To her left, a small glowing exit sign alerted her to the lobby door. Curling a hand around the knob, she yanked twice, meeting resistance.

Why wasn't it unlocked? This was the door they used during fire drills. Even before that thought fully penetrated, she put her feet into motion and bounded down the stairs heading to the basement.

The pepper spray Nick had mentioned came to mind. What she wouldn't give for some now.

At the bottom of the stairwell, Kylie whipped

her gaze around, although it was futile. The darkness, a deep black shrouded her view.

Her heart flailed against her rib cage. In the daylight she had a limited sense of direction and without lights she was clearly disoriented, but she kept her hand along the wall, palming her way in search of an escape route. Or even better, a place to hide.

Kylie blinked as the eerie gleam of a flashlight caught her eyes. Biting back a squeal, she dropped to a crouch, still moving. Still praying.

"You can't hide forever, Kylie, my girl." The man's muffled drawl carried through the darkness. Distorted, same as his phone calls.

Who was this maniac?

"Kylie, come out, come out wherever you are." The man's singsong voice echoed in her ears.

On second thought, she didn't want to know.

A stream of light flashed again, erratically zigzagging through the narrow space. Squeezing her lips tight to keep from making a sound, she stayed low. Her eyes followed the trail of the light. For a fleeting second it landed on a door a few yards away.

Hope expanded her chest.

Darkness fell again. A retreating set of footsteps echoed. The beam of light flashed in the opposite direction.

She had no time to lose. She crawled along the cold tile floor, mentally measuring the distance as she paused every two to three feet to feel out her surroundings. Finally her fingers brushed a doorknob.

Holding her breath, she clenched the knob and twisted it slowly, relieved that it wasn't locked. *Thank You, Lord!*

She wrenched the heavy door open just enough to slip inside. A loud clink boomed through the silence as the metal door slammed shut.

Frantically, she twisted the lock. Heavy footfalls echoed from outside.

Pulling out her cell phone, she used the light to probe the area.

The storage closet housed stacks of old chairs and file cabinets and other obsolete supplies.

"Kylie, I know you're in there." The doorknob rattled but the lock held. "I'm not going to hurt you." His voice sounded muffled and distorted and sent her blood pressure skyrocketing.

*Yeah, right.* Dropping everything, Kylie scrambled to one of the file cabinets. Mustering every ounce of her strength, she pressed against it, pushing the tall metal cabinet in front of the door.

Then, gathering her belongings, she crumpled onto a wooden pallet in the corner of the room and worked to catch her breath. As her heart squeezed out a silent prayer, her initial fears began to ebb. Either that or she was just too exhausted to care. She turned down the volume on her cell phone and punched in 911. She updated the dispatcher, praying the police wouldn't take long.

Then she keyed in Nick's number.

Nick picked up right away. She breathed easier. "Nick—"

Before she could get another word out, he started rambling. "Sorry. A cashier had an issue with the cash register, and I got tied up helping him. But I'll be there in a moment. You can't believe what kind of day I had—"

"Nick. Please listen," Kylie whispered, trying to keep her voice steady.

"Kylie, what's wrong?"

"I'm in the basement of the newspaper building. There's a door leading in from the parking lot."

"The basement? What are you doing there?"

"My stalker…the serial killer…he's here."

"What?"

"I locked myself in a storage room."

"Did you call the police?"

Kylie swiped at the perspiration prickling her brow. "Yes, they should be on their way."

"I'm almost at your office now. Is the stalker still there?"

A fist pounded on the door.

Her heart lurched. Panic rose again. "Yes!"

# TWELVE

Nick flew into the lot, tires squealing against the asphalt. Slamming on the brakes, he parked and jumped out of Kylie's car, still on the phone with a 911 operator. "Ma'am, Kylie Harper already called, but I just want to reiterate that she's in the basement of the *Asheville Daily News* building and the police need get over here now!"

Racing across the parking lot, he glanced right, then left, his gaze sweeping along the length of the brick building like a searchlight. Where was that door?

Toward the east side of the property, the land began to veer off, the slope becoming steep. Frustration rising, he stopped, assessed the scene, made a decision. He headed into a thick stretch of forest. He elbowed past bushes and fir trees as twigs and underbrush snapped beneath his boots, and made his way to the back of the building.

In his mind's eye Kylie's face appeared. He mentally kicked himself for being late. Once again, he'd let her down. Like he had Conrad.

He'd been dropped into the heaviest war zones in the world. He'd saved lives, made a difference. Home in Asheville, he was nothing more than a hazard.

Gnashing his teeth, Nick forced his brain off that track. No time for self-pity.

Through the trees he spotted a small parking lot and beyond that the building's loading dock, with several large metal overhead doors. Was that what Kylie had been talking about?

His question was answered as he broke into the clearing and caught a glimpse of the security door lost in the afternoon shadows.

He lengthened his stride, making for the door.

At the sound of keys jingling, Kylie shot to her feet. The lock rattled. Her nerves were back on alert.

This man had to be someone who worked for the paper. One of her colleagues.

A second passed; the doorknob twisted and creaked.

Heart in her throat, she threw her weight against the file cabinet as the heavy door cracked open, meeting resistance.

"Kylie, sweet Kylie, you are making this difficult."

*No kidding.* Pressing a shoulder to the cabinet, she strained, pushing with all her might as the man on the other side of the door used his strength to push against her.

For several long moments the reverse tug-of-war continued. As she made a desperate attempt to hold her ground, the heel of her shoe caught on a crack in the concrete floor. Her foot slipped and she thudded onto her hands and knees. Reacting fast and breathing hard, Kylie regained her footing, but not before the cabinet slid into the room several inches.

A distorted chuckle filled the air. Her heart leaped and she gulped for air.

With adrenaline spurring her on, she braced herself, threw her weight against the cabinet again and pushed harder.

At the back entrance to the building, Nick yanked on the metal knob once and when the security door didn't budge, he switched gears. He'd broken into more secure buildings than this, although not without the help of explosives. Still, he knew what he had to do.

Grabbing a wooden plank from the landing dock, he used it as a battering ram. Repeatedly, he thrust the blunt end of the lumber against the door lock. Pieces of metal cracked and shards flew in every direction. Using his pocketknife, Nick ripped loose the remnants of the handle, tossing them to the side.

A moment later, he pulled the door open. No alarm sounded. So much for security.

Light filtered through the doorway, breaking up the darkness and affording him a look around before he made his next move. Ahead of him, the small hallway ended and split into three directions. He took a step, listening closely. Two more steps and he heard a muffled sound to his right.

Nick flattened his back to the wall and moved slowly, carefully along the painted brick to the end of the hall. Instinctively, he ran a hand over the holster on his belt where he kept his revolver. Instead of his gun, his fingers wrapped around the leather case of his cell phone. Not a surprise, but his heart still sank a little.

He poked his head around the corner. A crack split the air. He pulled back as the whistle of a bullet shot past him. This guy wasn't playing.

Nick took a moment and thought how to proceed. No weapon. No backup—yet. He cupped his hand around his mouth and shouted, "Law enforcement is on the way. Do yourself a favor and give up now!"

Not really a threat, but he wanted the guy to do something crazy, make a mistake.

Another bullet whizzed through the air, echoing around the dead air.

Adrenaline scorched through Nick like wildfire. He wanted this guy.

Dropping to the floor, he belly crawled out into the corridor and made his way deeper into the building.

Seconds ticked by, but nothing happened, then another burst of gunfire rang out. Nick rolled several times, halting when he got to the entranceway of a closed office. He pulled himself up to one knee. "Give it up, creep!"

Silence. Then another shot sprayed toward him, burrowing into the wall beside his head.

Pulling back, he wedged himself into the narrow entranceway and caught his breath.

Retreating footsteps followed.

Nick kept his back plastered to the wall and waited an interminable length of time. Gradually, the footfalls faded. Then he got to his feet. His gut told him the coward was on the run. No great shock.

But what had he done with Kylie?

Fear raced through him. Nick hoped his tardiness hadn't caused Kylie any harm, or worse—

Gritting his teeth, he refused to allow his mind to stray in that direction.

Heart hammering, Nick edged into the main corridor, keeping his back flush to the wall just in case he was wrong and the killer was hanging around to finish the job. Dimness bled into darkness as he moved down the hallway.

Sirens blared in the distance, announcing the arrival of the police. If Kylie's stalker was still around, he'd heard them, too. Then it hit him. The creep probably had gotten away.

Frustration wrenched in Nick's chest, but he kept moving, curling his fingers into his palm. No matter what, he would find this guy. If not today, soon. Very soon.

Halting a moment, Nick took a chance and hollered, "Kylie!"

Silence answered him. No bullets. No Kylie. He took out his cell, dialed her number. No service. He had to be in a dead zone.

As lights flickered on, voices shouting orders came from behind him, along with footsteps thudding down the hallway. A glance over his shoulder caught three vested police officers rushing toward him, weapons drawn.

Nick gestured up ahead to the opposite end of the corridor. "I heard him running in that direction." His hand itched to curl his fingers around his revolver. He'd never thought he'd miss carrying a weapon.

Then again, he'd never thought he'd be chasing after murderers again.

One officer nodded as the trio scurried past him down one corridor and veered off into another.

"Where's Kylie?" Dave trailed the others, out of breath.

"Don't know. But I'm going to find her." Nick started moving again.

"I don't think that's wise, Nick. You're not even armed. This guy could be dangerous."

A fact Nick was well aware of. He stopped, glanced back. "I'm not walking out of here without her, Dave."

Dave caught up with him, tapped his holster. "I'll be right with you."

"Thanks." Nick picked up his pace. Not that it made much difference. He knew the mind of a psychopath. If there was a way out of there, this guy was long gone. He wasn't about to give up willingly. Escaping added to his adrenaline rush. This kind of criminal had to be caught in the act.

Kylie thanked God that at the sound of crashing metal, her pursuer gave up on trying to bust into the room. She finally managed to barricade the door again. This time more securely, using every article of furniture she could physically move. Having the lights on made things easier.

She leaned against one of the cabinets, swiping driblets of sweat from her brow and willing her pulse into submission. Her energy was about sapped, a complete contradiction to her racing heart rate.

Silence in the air settled around her. Several minutes had passed since she'd heard the last shot. It unnerved her to think the shots might have been aimed at Nick. She prayed he was safe. And as much as she longed to pick up her cell and call him, she wouldn't dare for the fear of giving away his position.

Terrible dread washed over her. What if Nick wasn't hiding? What if one of the bullets had hit him?

Her legs suddenly felt like pudding. She steadied herself against the cabinet. *Lord, please protect him. And get us both out of here.*

"Kylie!"

A distant voice echoed.

Hurriedly, she clambered up one chair to another and then on top of one of the cabinets, pressing her ear to the metal door. She wasn't about to respond to just anyone.

The call came again. Her heart leaped. It was Nick.

"I'm in here!" She pounded on the door.

Seconds later a heavy fist thumped on the opposite side. "Kylie, are you in there?"

"Yes." She shimmied down the side of the cabinet and twisted the lock. "I have the door barricaded. Hold on for a few minutes. I need to get everything out of the way."

"Okay. I'm right here waiting for you."

She couldn't be more grateful for that. She got right to work and as she pushed the last heavy cabinet out of the way, the door flew open. Tears of relief nearly blinded her as she ran to Nick and fell into his arms.

Outside the air was thick with humidity, the hum of katydids competing with chirping crickets and the distant banter of the law-enforcement officers from three counties that combed the adjacent forest and surrounding area.

Nick stood beside Kylie in the parking lot, surrounded by more people than he cared to count. Dave was among the other nameless police detectives, sheriff's deputy investigators and county inspectors, some in uniform, some not. Even Kylie's boss, Max, had felt the need to race over to lend moral support when he heard the news.

And the press had also arrived in droves to capture the latest news on Asheville's serial killer or spring butcher—two titles Kylie's stalker now officially owned.

Nick thumped his temple against a brewing headache. The gang was all here.

For the umpteenth time, Kylie recounted her twenty minutes of terror.

Nick caught her glance and sent her a reassuring smile. She looked as exhausted as he felt.

For the past hour the team of officers had drilled her. Questions came from all around; every investigator in the circle took their turn, surmising, inquiring, rephrasing, and from the beginning until now, Kylie's account had never changed. Long story short, she hadn't seen the shooter and, no, she would not be able to pick him out in a lineup.

Nick looked around, scowling when he realized how off track the conversation had gotten. They were hypothesizing what type of shoes the psychopath might have been wearing.

On Nick's list of priorities, this was way down the list. They hadn't found one footprint at either crime scene for the two murder victims. Only one pressing question mattered: Who was that psychopath?

"Why don't we concentrate on who had access to the building?" Nick piped up, trying to redirect the conversation. "Besides employees, there has to be security, janitorial services and probably dozens more."

All eyes swiveled toward him. Nick pulled back his shoulders and cleared his throat. As long as he had their attention, he'd wrap things up. He looked at Max. "Do you have a list of people that have been given the code or had keys issued to the building?"

Max shrugged. "I'm sure there has to be one. I'll check with security."

"Good." Nick shifted his gaze. "Dave, what time frame are we looking at before the forensic team will have the data on the bullets?"

Dave's shrug was tight. "A day or two, usually. But I plan to put a rush on it."

"Perfect." Now they were getting somewhere. "Well, unless you guys find something lurking inside or around the building, I guess we're at an impasse until then."

The law-enforcement officers met each other's eyes, passing agreeable nods and pocketing their notebooks.

"That's true." Dave scratched the side of his head with his pen. "Kylie, do you need anything from us? Or do you feel like you're safe enough where you're staying?"

Kylie rubbed at her bare forearms. The sun was setting; she was probably getting chilled. "Yeah, I'm fine. I'll be with Nick."

Nick shrugged off his jacket as his heart thumped against his sternum. She trusted him, probably too much. Guilt gripped his chest. Remorse wasn't a new phenomenon when it came to Kylie. He hated that he'd let her down before and now he'd done it again.

"Here you go." He draped his jacket over her shoulders.

Thick, long lashes fluttered up at him. "Thank you." She pulled the jacket tighter around her, a gentle softness in her feminine tone.

Not a bit of resentment in her voice. If God really did send blessings, Kylie's forgiving spirit would be his.

"Okay, Kylie, if you don't need anything from us, I guess we're done. You know where to reach me." Dave's voice drew him back.

Pushing hair away from her face, Kylie smiled. "Thanks, Dave."

Dave nodded, and then his gaze swung to Nick. "I'll update you as information comes in."

"Thank you." Nick appreciated Dave more and more.

Even after a horrendous day like this one, Kylie could still be pleasant. Nick wasn't feeling so generous. Every inch of him ached to track down her stalker and put this whole nightmare behind them. In the field he'd learned to wait and be patient. But once things started rolling, they zeroed in, took control. They were still at first base with this guy.

The group started to disperse.

"Kylie, don't forget your next article is due by midnight." Max threw her one of those geeky smiles.

Nick shook his head. So much for the moral-support theory.

Halfway across the parking lot, Dave braked to a stop, did an about-face. His bushy eyebrows shot up as he pointed a finger at Max. "Remember, Dawson, this is an ongoing investigation and I don't want anything in print that will jeopardize this case."

"Understood." Max raised a finger, pointing back at Dave. "However, Detective, I think it might be interesting if we look at some of the unsolved murders in North Carolina and see if we can tie this monster to any of them. If he killed Conrad Miller ten years ago, chances are there are other victims."

"This guy is bigger than life already," Dave snapped. "Right now my priority is to catch this criminal before he kills again. The last thing I need is more speculation out there. Let's concentrate on what we know."

Bravo. Nick liked it when Dave showed a little

emotion. "Thank you, Detective. I totally agree. Let's get this guy off the street before he gets any closer to Kylie."

Max shook his head. "I agree this creep needs to be caught, although—"

"Please, Max." Kylie jumped in smoothly. "Giving out possible credit for crimes this guy didn't commit will only boost his ego. I agree, we shouldn't stray in that direction yet."

"Listen to the lady." Dave grunted the order, then stalked away toward the collaborating investigators.

Max shifted and addressed Kylie. "Okay. Then how about raising the question—" he hooked his fingers, making air quotes "—'the Asheville Stalker: How bloodthirsty is he?'"

Kylie shook her head. "Max, you're beginning to sound like a tabloid editor."

"Hey, if you have a good alien story, I'm ready for it."

"For now, I'll concentrate on what happened today." She glanced at Nick. "Should be enough to hold the public's interest, don't you agree?"

Nick gave a sharp nod. "It certainly got my attention." He gestured to the other media hounds stalking the area. "And theirs."

"Okay, Kylie. Report what you know and don't forget to pour some emotion into it. Readers love that." Max threw her a wink.

Clenching his jaw, Nick used every bit of restraint to hold back from telling Max to shut his mouth. This ordeal was stressful enough without him putting more pressure on Kylie.

"Okay, Max," Kylie conceded. "I'll work on the story tonight."

If nothing else, Kylie was reliable. Maybe even a little too accommodating to that boss of hers.

Leaving the lower parking lot, Kylie hiked back with Nick through the forested patch. The sidewalk leading around the building was blocked off by police barricades and she had no interest in walking back through the building.

It felt like a breath of fresh air once they cleared the trees and emerged into the main parking area, leaving behind the horrors of the afternoon.

Kylie squinted against the slowly sinking sun and spotted Max across the lot. He raised his hand, sending her a quick salute. His patented farewell.

She gave a quick wave back, relieved to be finally leaving for the day.

"And to think I actually thought I might be wrong about him," Nick said, falling into step bedside her as they headed for the car. "But after those last few comments he made today, I have a higher opinion of pond scum."

Kylie looked at Nick. His narrowed gaze appeared to be roving the parking area. If anyone was going to catch her stalker, it would be him. In the meantime, she still didn't buy his theory that her editor might be the killer.

A cool breeze picked up, brushing against Kylie's cheeks. She gathered the collar of the jacket closer, staving off a shiver. "You have to understand Max. Being a chief editor is a painstaking job. It's his position to sell newspapers. He's constantly on the lookout for new talent and quality stories. Whether it is a human-interest story or breaking news, it doesn't matter as long as it attracts the reader."

"And in the process he'll sacrifice one of his employees to sell papers?"

Biting her lip, Kylie thought about that. "Well, maybe. But not intentionally."

A bark of laughter resounded. "I'll take that as a yes."

Kylie sighed. "I know you consider him a suspect. But as aggressive as he seems, he's harmless."

Nick's skeptical gaze barely touched on her before he pulled open the car door. "There is a school of thought that safety comes first. I wonder if he's ever heard of it."

Kylie smiled. "Heard of it? Or believes it?"

He matched her smile. "I figured as much."

She slipped into the passenger seat and Nick circled the car and got in. Before turning on the ignition, he sat a moment, his lips pursed as if he was pondering the situation.

"What's wrong?"

He glanced over at her, an incredulous, rather concerned look darkening his gaze. "You realize this killer isn't lurking in the shadows. He's probably watching us now."

Kylie drew in a deep breath. "As much as I hate to consider that, I'm sure you're right. I just wish I had a gut feeling on who this guy is."

Nick's glare didn't waver. "You need to start looking over your shoulder a little more. You can't discount anyone, not even Max."

Kylie nodded. "I'm going to pay closer attention to everything happening around me. If I find anything even a little out of the ordinary, I'll make sure to let Dave know."

"Good." Nick flashed her a smile. "You're getting into that investigative-reporter mind-set. Push emotions aside. Focus on the facts."

As if that was easy. She tried for a confident smile.

"This guy is getting too close to you for my comfort and we need to get this thing wrapped up before he gets any closer. I want you safe and sound when I leave here."

Nick cranked up the motor and pulled out of the parking lot. His protective instincts astounded her. He was concerned about her safety not because he loved her, but to ease his conscience.

Unable to look at him, Kylie lolled back against the leather seat and curled her hands in her lap.

Staring out the window, she watched the sun sink into the tree line as swiftly as her battered heart shriveled in her chest.

A small, rational part of her pointed out that Nick had loved her once, but had since moved on. And, she reminded herself, so had she. At least that was what she'd thought, until he'd showed up again.

Now one look into his eyes and she was tempted to forget all the reasons she couldn't allow herself to love him again. Forget the hurt and sadness that lingered long after he was gone.

Pressure built in Kylie's chest. She took a slow breath to ease it. Nick had been the last person she'd thought would break her heart. And he had the ability to do it again.

Something she couldn't let happen.

She felt the heat of his glance, caught it with her peripheral vision but refused to meet his gaze.

"Are you feeling okay?"

She nodded, afraid of what she might say if she spoke. It wasn't his fault that love and regret from the past still had power over her.

"Sit back and rest. I know it's been a long day."

She nodded again. He was right. She was exhausted...nearly as much as she was confused. But logical thoughts were sure to come. Even if she only half believed that rationale, she tilted her head back, closed her eyes and let the soft music filling the car relax her.

# THIRTEEN

Later that evening, still hyped up from the chaos of the day, Nick and Kylie collapsed in the living room. Nick took the sofa and Kylie curled beneath a blanket on the adjacent love seat. They finally had a moment to breathe, to regroup.

Earlier, after arriving back at his brother's house, Kylie worked on her article and he'd spent some time brainstorming trying to link the few clues they had.

Not a productive venture. So many questions still hung in the air.

That realization deflated him some.

And he was already exhausted. It had been a while since he'd dodged gunfire and he'd never been less prepared. A precarious situation he didn't care to repeat. Especially since he didn't have a permit to carry a handgun in North Carolina, let alone conceal one.

Nonetheless, he was glad the shots had been aimed at him and not Kylie.

Planting his socked feet on the coffee table, he tried to erase the surreal events swirling in his brain. He pressed the remote and the movie previews started.

This wasn't how things used to be. Him on one couch, Kylie on another.

He sneaked a glance at her, curious if she might be thinking the same thing. Her eyes were focused on the TV. Her neutral expression gave him no clue.

The movie trailers continued on the flat screen. Usually he'd fast-forward to the opening scene, but for now he chose to sit back and wait. He was enjoying the quiet moments, being there with Kylie, his mind engrossed in nothing more than memories.

A dangerous proposition. But for the next few minutes he'd allow the indulgence.

"What movie did you finally decide on?" Kylie's question broke through his thoughts.

Nick crossed his arms and tried to remember. "Can't recall the name. Some chick flick. I thought you might enjoy that."

"Really? You picked out a *chick* flick?" She met his gaze, fluttering long, full lashes that fringed her wide eyes. They exchanged smiles.

"Actually, I can't take the credit. Steven's the movie buff. I asked him for ideas—something with a good plot, but not too sappy."

"That was nice of you, and Steven. Thank you."

"You're welcome. Somehow I got the impression a crime or murder mystery wouldn't be very relaxing for you tonight." He winked at her and grinned.

Her eyes widened farther. "Very true."

Linking his hands behind his head, he settled

more comfortably against the leather cushions. "Now all we're missing is a mug of hot chocolate and popcorn."

Another smile flickered on Kylie's lips. "You remember that?"

He crossed one ankle over the other and surveyed her with narrowed eyes. How could he forget? Snuggled up beside the most beautiful girl in Asheville, sipping a marshmallow-topped chocolaty brew while munching on fresh, buttery popcorn. All under the watchful eye of her father.

He couldn't stop a smile. No stolen kisses those nights. Still, priceless memories.

"Sure do. You made some killer hot chocolate back then. Real milk and everything, right?"

Kylie straightened in her seat, eyes bright. "That's right. Cocoa, sugar, the works. The milk in Steven's refrigerator is about gone, but I'm sure he must have a couple instant packets of hot cocoa somewhere in his pantry. Maybe even some microwave popcorn."

"Good enough. What are we waiting for?" Nick surged to his feet and Kylie rose right beside him. He pressed Pause on the remote and they headed into the kitchen.

It actually took fifteen minutes to locate the hot drink, stuffed between packages of instant oatmeal. And the popcorn was well hidden in the vegetable bin inside the refrigerator, of all places.

Nick grabbed two mugs from the cabinet while Kylie filled the kettle and set it to boil on the stove.

After collecting butter and a shaker of salt, he set the timer on the microwave and pressed Start. "I need to have a talk with Steven. I found some gold bullion coins in his top dresser drawer today, yet he keeps hot chocolate hidden in his pantry."

Leaning against the counter, Kylie laughed. "I've always loved Steven. He has such a grip on what's important."

"Yep." Nick nodded. "He certainly has his own list of priorities. His quest for a wife being number one at the moment."

"Any luck with Amy, his physical therapist?"

"Actually, he's moved on to Nadine, his nurse."

Kylie's eyes rounded. "Wow, popular guy."

"He seems to have his pick at the moment. And he's confident his days as a bachelor will be over by year's end. The interesting part is he doesn't have an inkling who Mrs. Right will even be."

"Scary. What's his hurry?"

"Beats me." Nick shrugged. He'd wondered the same thing. Marriage was a big step. A promise for forever. At least that was what Nick would want if he ever took the plunge.

"How about you, Kylie? If Mr. Right came along, would you be ready?"

Instantly, Kylie blanched. Her gaze clung to his and he saw her bottom lip quiver.

*Oops.* Sore subject. Nick inwardly groaned. "Sorry. Too personal."

"No. It's just that I don't know how to answer a question like that. I suppose I'll have to see when Mr. Right actually gets here." Kylie's lips pressed in a firm line even as color began to rise back into her delicate cheeks.

Pummeled with a tidal wave of regret, Nick exhaled to release the tightness in his chest. He wasn't Mr. Right, of course, but deep down, he'd hoped she once thought he might have been.

Egotistical and probably not at all what Kylie would think. But whoever said emotions made sense?

"Understood." He masked his discomfort with a smile.

The look in Kylie's eyes grew tender. Was it the flicker of the light that made the jade-and-white rays in her irises shimmer like that?

His throat knotted with emotion. As he swallowed, the temptation to walk over and kiss her overpowered every other thought.

Not wise. Enough pain had passed between them. He didn't dare propagate more.

Still, he found it difficult to douse the longing that heated through his veins. But as he looked into Kylie's eyes, the intensity of her gaze sent a shock wave through his nervous system, igniting his synapses with enough electricity to light up all of Asheville. He drew a step closer, stopping himself just shy of touching her.

He'd made mistakes in his life, but pushing Kylie away had topped the list. Too late to go back—he knew that.

"Kylie, if anything had happened to you today, I would never have forgiven myself. I'm so glad you're okay." His voice dipped several octaves, emotion that surprised even him.

"Forgive yourself?" her soft voice echoed. "You showed up just in time. Being there probably saved my life. Something I will always be grateful for."

At the slightly baffled expression flitting across her face, he clarified, "If I hadn't been late to pick you up, that horrendous episode could have been avoided."

Kylie stared openmouthed at him as if he'd just morphed into some dopey-looking cartoon character.

He narrowed an eye on her. "Don't you get what I'm trying to say?"

"Nick, you're not my caretaker. You aren't responsible for what happens to me. Just like you weren't responsible for what happened to Conrad. You're one person. Not some herculean superhuman."

Good. A better comparison then a cartoon.

He cleared his throat. "It's not that easy, Kylie. My presence today would have saved you some grief, and ten years ago…well, we've beaten that horse enough."

She shot up her hand, palm out. "*Might have* is the key phrase here, not *would have*. Life happens and not always according to plan, even if everyone is where they're supposed to be."

To some degree she made sense. Nick gave a shrug. "Something to consider. Although it feels a bit like a cop-out."

Kylie just shook her head.

Nick leaned in, caught her gaze. "I've let people down that I care about, Kylie. I don't know how to undo that."

"You're sorry. You made amends," she said softly. The wounded look in her eyes nearly broke his heart. In the midst of his other mistakes, he'd caused her that pain.

If he could do it over again, things would be so much different.

"The past can't be changed, Nick. Only the future." Kylie's gaze was intent on his face. She skimmed her fingertips along the edge of his jaw. "You don't have to live like this."

A future filled with fear. Fear of losing someone else he cared about. Fear of more mistakes. No. He didn't want to live like that. But saying it and doing it were two different things.

Tears glistened in Kylie's eyes. She withdrew her fingers, but she stayed where she was. So close he marked every breath, the rhythm of her respirations, the measured beat of her pulse against the hollow of her throat.

"Life is too short, too precious. You have to let go," she whispered, her passion evident. She almost had him sold until more memories crowded his mind, haunting reminders.

His heart gave a thump. "Conrad's life was snuffed out before he was even a man. How can I let go of that?"

"It's not your fault."

"Then whose fault is it, Kylie? You don't blame God. Someone has to be responsible."

She huffed softly. "There's a maniac on the loose. He's the culprit, not you. Can't you understand that?"

"I'd like to understand. I'd like to place the burden on him and let go of that night. But I can't."

"So you're willing to give up everything, your life included, just to remain a martyr?"

That sounded harsh. Still, Nick had to admit there might be some truth in what she said. But if forgiving himself was the only way to find happiness, he was sure to die a lonely man.

He brushed a lone tear from her cheek. "Not a martyr, Kylie. Just a guilty soul."

And baring his soul tonight gave him an odd sense of freedom. At least when it came to Kylie Harper. He'd carried that burden too long.

"I was like you once, Nick." Kylie sniffed. "After Conrad died and you left, I was hurt, too.

For months I cried with guilt and regret while the rest of the town managed to heal. Finally, God gave me the peace that I longed for. That's when I forgave myself for something I wasn't responsible for in the first place."

Nick listened to her words. She made it sound so easy.

"You believed once, Nick."

His faith had slipped away along with his dreams of a future with Kylie. God was a part of a past that no longer existed.

"Please, for your own sake, get right with God. Let Him heal you. Let Him give you back the life that you're sacrificing." She paused, moistening her lips.

Nick couldn't stop himself. He slipped his arm around her waist. Kylie inhaled, but instead of pulling away, she leaned closer. He caught the scent of her sweet perfume.

Ignoring the warning bells in his brain, he slid his thumb up over her chin and back into her hair. On a shaky sigh, Kylie parted her lips, but didn't speak.

Still cupping her face, he leaned in and kissed her on the cheek, then on the tip of her nose. As his lips hovered over hers, he whispered, "You know I'll always care—"

Kylie's hand came between them. She pressed her fingers over his lips, halting the words. "Don't say any more, Nick. You have no plans for a future here. No future with me."

The whistle of the teakettle lit the air and shattered the moment.

Pulling away, Nick turned and switched off the stove.

When he turned back to Kylie, she was busy with the popcorn, pouring it in the bowl.

Regret and sorrow hit like a sucker punch in his gut. He mentally kicked himself for letting his guard down and crossing the line of their friendship.

Inappropriate and pointless. No matter how hard he tried, he could never be the person he once was.

As midnight rolled around, Kylie shifted her position on the love seat, trying to stay focused on the movie, which was quickly becoming an unbearable undertaking. A cute love story about reunited lovers. Just what she didn't need tonight.

She blew out a sigh.

An action adventure or thriller sounded better all the time.

*True love only happens in the movies.* She ignored the cynical thought. She hadn't completely given up on love, but also couldn't ignore the man on the next sofa, who was more prepared to run than pick up the pieces of their life and start all over again.

A gentle snore escaped Nick. With arms folded

across his chest and feet propped on the coffee table, he looked way too relaxed for someone with so many regrets.

And those regrets were making her life miserable.

Shaking off the dark thoughts, Kylie centered her attention on the movie, but not before a wave of emotion burned in her eyes.

Nick held the guilt of Conrad's death like a man trying to hold up a burning building, clinging to the very thing that would destroy him.

And she couldn't help him with that battle he fought within himself.

A fist tightened around her heart. She needed to keep that fact in the forefront of her mind. She couldn't change Nick Bentley.

Closing her eyes, she lifted a prayer for God's mercy in his life.

"Is the movie over already?"

Kylie's eyes blinked open. Straightening in her seat, she glanced over at the TV, surprised to see he was right. "I guess it is."

"So you were dozing, too?"

Biting her lip, she looked back at him. "Just resting."

Actually pouting, but she'd spare him that information.

"That good, huh?" he asked with a coltish grin.

A story about love, joy and a happy ending. A

little too good at the moment. "It was enjoyable. I've just had a long day."

"No kidding." Nick dropped his feet to the floor, tilted forward and picked up his full mug of now-cold chocolate. He took a sip.

Kylie stared at him. "I can heat that up for you."

"No thanks. Chocolate is chocolate." He gave a satisfied sigh.

Kylie shook her head. What was it about men that one moment they could be heavyhearted, bare their souls, and the next moment they were care-free and amusing?

Here she was still mulling over the conversation they'd had in the kitchen and Nick's thoughts were already on new things. Probably his next grand adventure to who knew where.

Kylie drew in a cleansing breath and let it out slowly. No wonder men found women so complicated.

"So tell me about the movie."

Nick's question pulled her back. She blinked. "Well—" Kylie faltered, her teeth sinking into her lower lip. "It was about love and, well…love."

He canted his head. "More sappy than I thought. But I'm glad you enjoyed it."

Actually, she wished she could have slept through it, too.

Nick settled back on the sofa, his drink in his hand. "What's on your agenda for tomorrow?"

"After work, I was thinking about going to visit my parents. There's a direct flight at six-thirty."

About to swallow more cocoa, he nearly choked on his question. "What?"

Kylie shrugged. "It's been a while since I've seen them and I'm up for some beachy sunshine. And I'm sure you need a break."

Nick lowered his cup. "We've talked about this. You can't leave. We need to get this stalker issue resolved before you go anywhere."

Her stalker wasn't the only issue she needed to resolve. The ping-pong of emotions she experienced with this very gentleman was quite draining. Maybe not to the same degree as the lunatic in the building today. But close.

Kylie knotted her fingers in her lap to keep from wringing her hands. Nick was making her crazy. He'd dropped back into her life, turned her emotions upside down and now had the nerve to sit there and act like a friend after nearly kissing her in the kitchen.

A combination of anger and sadness welled up in her chest. Inhaling deeply for calm, she managed to breathe through it. "I need a break. My parents live in a gated community. Even if the stalker followed, I think I'd be safe."

"Not true, Kylie." A frown marred Nick's good looks. He sat up and placed his mug on the coffee table. Leaning forward, he rested his arms on his knees. "I told you before, you're not safe anywhere. It's best to hang around Asheville and get this thing resolved. Your stalker is bound to get sloppy and I have a gut feeling that we're getting close to finding him."

His prediction should have made her feel relieved. But instead her heart pinched harder. After the danger was out of her life, Nick would be also. He'd walk away and not look back, just like before. But this time, she feared, the void would leave a permanent hole in her heart.

She met his gaze, wishing he could read her thoughts. He stared back, concern instead of understanding in his gaze. She swallowed. "You're probably right. But if this keeps on much longer, I'm out of here."

He nodded. "Deal."

Not a threat or a warning, but a promise. The more time she spent with Nick, the harder it would be to say goodbye.

She got to her feet. Exhaustion burned in every muscle. She needed sleep. "I better get to bed." Tomorrow was a new day. Hopefully, her heart and her head would be more in sync.

Her pulse slowed. Nothing about her tomorrows looked promising.

Thanks to Nick Bentley.

Nick checked his wristwatch, yawning. "It is late. It's almost one." He saluted her with his mug. "Sweet dreams. I'll see you in the morning."

Kylie trudged to her room, ready to collapse in

the bed. If she had one dream come true in her life, she'd wish for Nick to get out of his rut, forgive himself and start over in Asheville.

Such a simple dream, but one that tore her heart to shreds.

# FOURTEEN

Amazing what a little sleep could do. Kylie felt refreshed. Tucking the horrors of the day before in the darkest corner of her mind, she set about organizing her desk in the newsroom. Papers and note scraps littered the top, a plethora of information she needed to sort through. She hardly knew where to begin. With all the latest breaking news, she'd gotten behind on her other projects.

"Great article. Headline story again."

Kylie glanced over her shoulder to find Max stalking toward her, waving the front-page section of the newspaper around like a cheerleader shaking a pom-pom.

"Every press syndicate in the good ole U. S. of A. wants dibs on this story. Our little newspaper has finally caught the attention of the big boys. Whoop, whoop." He sounded like a wounded chimp.

Hoots and whistles from her fellow journalists followed, filling the newsroom. Max indulged them with a mock bow before sending off a saucy salute. "Thank you. Thank you. Although I can't take all the credit. This wouldn't have been possible without Miss Harper here." He made a sweeping gesture toward Kylie.

Shaking her head, Kylie almost laughed, despite the crazy truth. People were dying and Max was celebrating the news.

When the cheers and laughing subsided, Max plunked down in a chair across from her desk.

Although the banter had been in jest, she could almost see his head swell.

Maybe there was some merit to Nick's concerns about her boss. He was enjoying the paper's new-found celebrity status a little too much.

Even his crooked smile looked a little more dastardly than usual. The last time she'd seen him this happy was when he bought his used Porsche at the sheriff's repo auction.

*Making good on the misfortune of others.* She'd thought he was kidding at the time.

Kylie glanced over at him and studied his cheeky smile. Maybe not.

She swallowed. "The town is swarming with media. I can't believe other newspaper syndicates are willing to pay for my coverage."

"You know townsfolk around here are leery about outsiders. Law enforcement is staying equally tight-lipped. You're right in the middle of the mayhem—every other journalist is reporting from the sidelines. Even we can't convey all the gory details, but theirs takes a backseat to your bird's-eye view."

"You mean duck-in-hunting-season view, but I see what you're saying."

Max howled. "Good one, Kylie."

She wasn't kidding.

Frankly, she was tired of talking about the horrors of yesterday. It was bad enough that with every undistracted moment, visions of the ordeal emerged in her head, bringing with them a shiver of panic. For just a little while she wanted to forget, not have the Asheville murders front and center in her mind.

Jiggling the mouse, she brought the computer out of hibernation mode and then gathered her notes and shoved a pencil behind her ear. Hopefully, Max would get the hint.

"Well, it looks like you're busy, so I won't waste any more of your time."

*Thank you.* "I'm running behind. The managing editor wants two articles before four o'clock."

"You better get to work, then. Charlie doesn't like to be kept waiting. And I know how tough his boss can be." He winked and slipped out the newsroom door.

Kylie got busy, excited to redirect her focus on state-fair animals and a ninety-nine-year-old resident's birthday celebration.

Thirty minutes later, her coworker Ron pointed to the doorway. "Kylie, I think there's someone here to see you."

Swiveling in her seat, she offered a quick wave to Dave, who stood across the room, craning his neck, a searching look on his face.

When she caught his eye, he raised his dark

brows and nodded, then started toward her. Hope for a productive day was looking a little less promising.

"Morning, Kylie." Dave gave a clipped nod. "I'd like to speak to you, if you have a moment."

"Of course." Kylie pushed back her chair and got to her feet. "Is the employee lounge okay?"

Another nod.

She led the way through a maze of coworker desks to a small room behind the proofing office. On the way she introduced the detective to several colleagues, downplaying her anxiety about why he'd showed up unannounced. In the break room, the aroma of fresh-brewed coffee greeted them.

"Would you like to sit down?" She gestured to the chairs around a small table.

Dave shook his head. "No, thanks, I'll stand."

Kylie grabbed a cup from a dispenser on the wall. "How about some coffee?" She glanced over at him; his demeanor was hesitant.

"No, thank you."

Her body went rigid. Dave had come here with news and it didn't look good. She swallowed. "Do you mind if I have some?"

"That's fine."

Whirling around, she started to fix her drink, hoping Dave's visit wouldn't further rock her day. "Any word on the forensic reports from the bullets?"

"They came back this morning. The ammo

recovered was three nine-millimeter Luger cartridges, used in a Glock 17 handgun."

Kylie turned back and leaned against the counter, stirring her coffee with a plastic spoon. "That's good news, isn't it? You can see how many guns like that are registered around here and maybe—"

Dave gave a shake of his head before she even finished. "The Glock is the most popular revolver in America. They can be easily obtained with a license and without. Criminals pick them up every day on the street."

Her stomach quivered. "Are we still at square one with this guy?"

"That depends."

Kylie stopped stirring her coffee. "Depends on what?"

"You."

"Me?" Using the spoon, she aimed it at herself, sending droplets of russet liquid dribbling onto her shoe.

He gave an affirmative nod. "You never gave me those names I asked you for."

"Names?"

He sent her an unamused glance. "Names of possible love interests."

Her brain finally jumped into gear. "Oh, yes. Of course. I haven't had a chance to get one together yet." Before he could remind her how important it was, she added, "But I plan to work on it soon."

Dave's face was impassive, not that unusual for

him, but today his deadpan stare seemed to indicate she hadn't done enough to help them get the case solved. Surely he didn't think she enjoyed the chaos?

Kylie tossed the spoon into the trash. "I'll try to have the list to you by tomorrow."

"That will be good." His expression softened. "It's one avenue we haven't explored yet. Focus on high school. Maybe some guy that's kept in touch or goes out of his way to impress you or be around you."

"Okay." Kylie nodded, her mind drawing a blank. "Hard to believe this criminal is so good at being…well, a criminal."

Dave furrowed his forehead. "You still don't have a gut feeling about anyone?"

She gave a quick shrug and sighed. "No. Although," she amended, lowering her voice, "there is my boss, Max. He wasn't at the camp with us ten years ago, but he's well versed in the town's history and is really enjoying the notoriety of the story at the moment." As she reiterated Nick's suspicion, Dave lifted his brows and narrowed his gaze on her.

"Interesting. It's good to see that you're considering possible suspects."

"Actually, he's someone Nick is considering. I'm trying to keep an open mind."

"And what about Nick?"

She gave a short laugh. "I don't think anyone is safe from his scrutiny at the moment."

"That's not what I meant. I want to know what *you* think of Nick."

Kylie stared at Dave while shock and concern churned in her stomach. What was he getting at?

"Kylie?"

She blinked, then hesitated. "Well, I think Nick has been a great help to the investigation."

Dave's brows lifted and in that moment, she noticed his green eyes, nearly the shade of her own. She'd never paid much attention to them before. Then again, Dave rarely looked anyone in the eye. Now as he held her stare, her nerves skittered. The switch in his demeanor meant one thing— he felt strongly about something he wanted her to consider.

Then it hit her.

"Dave, you don't think—" Kylie stopped short, reeling at the insinuation in his features. "You can't possibly think Nick is involved with the murders."

Dave's gaze didn't waver. "Nick's been away from Asheville for ten years. He's a trained soldier and not immune to killing. He has access to intelligence information, making it easy to keep an eye on you over the years. He comes back and people start dying."

"If that were true, why would Nick take the time to kill other people when he has direct contact with me? He doesn't have to lure me anywhere. I'm staying in his brother's home."

"Games and control. It's not uncommon for a psychopath to con their victim, try to earn their trust before they go after them. And in the meantime, they enjoy the notoriety from the other crimes they commit."

Breaking his gaze, Kylie gasped to catch her breath. Dave's knowledge on this type of criminal paralleled Nick's. And she was beginning to understand way too much about the mind of a psychopathic murderer.

Nerves about shot now, a fine tremor ran through her. She slid her cup onto the counter, more worried about spilling her coffee then drinking it at the moment. "I don't understand why you would suspect Nick. Everything you have on him is circumstantial."

"Well, the clues are adding up. He was also the one who found Conrad the night he was murdered."

"That's not true." Kylie's heart jumped, the scene of Conrad's lifeless body sprawled across the cabin deck clearly in her mind.

"If I'm wrong, correct me about that night," Dave said, his voice firm, very detective-like.

*Breathe.*

Taking a moment, Kylie plucked her cup off the

counter and took a swig to add moisture to her dry throat. The whole conversation was ludicrous.

She lowered her cup, her wits returning. "I was with Nick that night. We found Conrad together."

Dave nodded. "I remember. You were on a walk while the rest of us were at the bonfire."

"Yes."

"How long were you gone?"

She shrugged. "An hour. Maybe an hour and a half."

"The coroner's report stated Conrad had been lying in his own blood for about that length of time before he was found."

"I don't remember hearing that."

Dave shrugged, his dull gaze lingering on her.

Kylie flapped a dismissive hand. "It doesn't matter anyway. Nick was with me. He had nothing to do with Conrad's death. I can attest to that." Her voice took on a defensive tone, but she didn't care.

"Did you meet at his cabin before you left on the walk?"

She stopped to think, to remember. Finally, she said, "No, he met me at mine."

Nodding, Dave tapped a foot. As if he was waiting for her to see the light.

Kylie drew herself up to her full five-foot-two-inch height. She popped a hand on her hip. Grasping for straws, that was what Dave was doing. And she'd had enough of this inquisition.

But Dave wasn't finished. "Whenever you've received a call from the stalker, has Nick been around?"

"No."

"Never?"

She cringed as the question slammed into her. One she had never considered. It did seem odd that most of the calls came when Nick was close by but not actually with her. He was always easy to reach afterward, as if he was waiting.

The sane corner of her mind told her to toss that last thought out.

Swallowing, she wanted to discount Dave's suspicions, but reasonably she couldn't. His words held some clout. Still, she understood the importance of remaining objective.

At any other time in her life, that might have been possible.

Her confusion must have showed. "Purely speculation at this point," Dave offered, his tone even, no emotion in his voice, but she knew what he was thinking.

She nodded. "I know you have to consider all options."

The pause before he answered her went on forever. When he finally cut her a glance, his eyes darkened. "We're narrowing down the pertinent facts. I'll keep you posted on any new developments." With one last dark glance, he walked out of the room.

Stunned, Kylie stood there, her heart lodged in her throat. *Lord, help me understand what is going on here.* First Max and now Nick. Could either of them be capable of murder?

Kylie ran stiff fingers through her curls, pulling her hair. She added to her prayer, *Give me wisdom and keep my mind clear.*

The workday was getting away from Nick again. He was quickly discovering that a good day's work took much longer than a single day. Appreciation for his brother's patience in running a business continued to grow.

"Nick, the last box is off the truck. I'll do a quick inventory and then take an early dinner."

"Thanks, Roger. That will be fine."

Nick stood in the stockroom, carefully examining the list of supplies that had been delivered. He didn't know what half of the stuff was, let alone where it belonged in the store. Hopefully, Roger wouldn't mind sticking around after his shift. Between Nick and the newer employees, they'd be here all night.

With a groan, he stuffed the list into one coat pocket and pulled his cell phone from the other.

He punched in Kylie's number. Hopefully, her day was going better than his.

Plunking down on a padded work stool, he waited for her to answer.

"Hello." Kylie's sweet voice floated over the line.

Refreshing. "Busy?"

"For about two more minutes."

"Two minutes?" He wished that was his case.

"I'm adding the finishing the touches to two overdue articles and emailing them to the managing editor. Hold on."

Nick waited. He swatted at a cobweb above him. Stretched his back, then scratched the side of his jaw where his cut was still healing.

Finally Kylie came back on the line. "I'm finally finished." Relief in her voice.

"Let's celebrate. I'll take you out to dinner tonight. Name the place."

Silence for a heartbeat. "Actually, I'm busy tonight." Her voice came back low, vibrating along his spine with an unexpected chill.

"Do you have another article to work on?"

"No, I'm meeting a friend for dinner. Someone from church."

Male or female? He didn't ask, but he was curious.

He had a ton of work to do, anyway. He should have been relieved, but he wasn't. "Okay. Since I have your car, I can pick you up and drive you to the restaurant."

"No, that's too much trouble. My friend will swing by here and then drop me off at Steven's afterward."

Nick steeled his spine. He'd be happy to drive her and he almost told her so, but he heard something in her voice that told him she didn't want him hanging around.

He cleared his throat. "Then I'll see you this evening. Any idea what time you'll be back—" The rest of the words stuck in his throat. He was sounding like a father, not like a friend.

A friend who had stepped over his boundaries the night before. He could kick himself.

"I'm not sure, but I still have the key that you gave me. Don't feel like you have to wait up."

Shock jolted down the nerves of his spine. He sloughed it off and straightened his shoulders. How late was too late for him to wait up? He bit back the question, reminding himself to mind his own business. "All right. Be safe."

Silence fell. Even more awkward this time. Nick shifted again.

Finally, she replied, "I will. Have a good night, Nick."

"You, too."

Although the likelihood of that happening now was about nil.

Strangely disappointed, Nick sat for a moment

after Kylie hung up. No big deal, he told himself. A little separation was good for both of them. She could see whomever she wanted. She had no allegiance to him.

Still, he'd been looking forward to seeing her.

Since he'd arrived, he'd been wrestling with past feelings for her. The chemistry was still there. A scary proposition that deep down inside he knew would lead nowhere.

His life was scattered enough without a relationship to hold him down, especially with no plans set in stone. He had no idea where he'd be next. His only concern for Kylie was to keep her safe. He repeated that thought over and over in his head, drilling it in. Rhetoric he vowed to hold on to.

Something caught in his chest. Right then and there, he decided to get a grip and grow up. He'd been home less than two weeks, and already he'd regressed to acting like a teen. A lovesick teen, at that.

"Hey, Nick. It looks like all the supplies we ordered came in. Here are the completed inventory sheets." Roger walked toward him and handed him a clipboard.

Blinking to align his jumbled thoughts, Nick cleared his throat and tried to grin. "Thanks."

He took the clipboard and tucked it under his arm. He'd compare it to the master list later. "Roger, would you be interested in working late tonight? If you'd like a few extra hours, I could use some help getting the supplies stocked in the right location."

A shrug from Roger. "Sure, I'm free. I don't have anyone to get home to."

*I know the feeling.* Nick groaned inside. "Okay. Get yourself some dinner and we'll get started when you get back."

"I'm ordering pizza. I'll make it a large if you'd like some?"

"Sure. Why not?" He had no one waiting at home for him, either.

# FIFTEEN

In the newsroom, Kylie leaned back, rocking lightly in her office chair. Lifting a hand, she rubbed at the headache thumping behind her left temple. It had been harder than she expected telling Nick she had other plans. And it didn't help that he'd invited her to dinner. A scenario she hadn't considered when she arranged to meet up with her friend Taylor.

But after Dave's surprise visit that morning, she needed a distraction. Some time to mull over the what-ifs and the maybes about the case. The suspicions Dave had raised about Nick sent her stomach into knots. And as much as she wanted to refute his theory, she couldn't deny her life had been rather peaceful until Nick showed up again.

For one ghastly, twisted moment, she imagined Nick Bentley as her stalker. The murderer of three innocent men.

Hurt and sadness sent achy chills twining through her like a bad case of the flu.

Repressing a shiver, she gritted her teeth. No. It couldn't be him.

Every fiber of her being strained to believe that. Confusion rattled her brain and intensified her pounding headache at the same time. Closing her eyes, she rubbed harder at her temple.

Regardless of everything else, Nick would be out of her life soon. It only made sense to pull away some, for self-preservation and to shore up her still-fragile heart.

"I just got off the phone with Charlie. He said you made the copy deadline. Congratulations."

At Max's words, Kylie's wayward thoughts jolted to a stop. Jerking upright in her chair, she whipped her gaze up to find him staring at her from across her desk, his usual smirk in place.

"You must be tired."

More than he could imagine. "It's been a long couple of weeks." She brushed hair from her face.

"Yes, but interesting to say the least." His crooked smile grew. "I've been thinking, after this crime is solved, you might consider selling your story for a book or maybe even movie rights. I'll be happy to represent you myself. I have a few friends in the publishing business."

His eyes rounded with enthusiasm and Kylie bit her tongue to keep from telling him to stop thinking.

She pushed up from her seat, and bracing her fingertips on the desktop, she leaned in and stared at Max.

Eyebrows drew together over the thrust of his

nose. Inching back a step, he asked, "What are you looking at?"

She canted her head, staring harder. "I wanted to get a good look at the dollar signs in your eyes."

Max's short bark of laughter bounced around the room, further enhanced by chuckles erupting from nearby coworkers.

Satisfied and fighting a grin, Kylie resumed her seat. "You know, you're making me crazy, Max."

He gave a shrug, still laughing. "Everyone has a job to do."

"You do yours well."

Another crooked smile sprouted. "Can I assume you don't want me to pitch your story to any of the publishers I know?"

"Correct."

"Okay, but if you change your mind, you know where to find me."

*Unfortunately.*

He shot her his infamous two-finger salute and walked out of the newsroom.

As far as Max being her stalker, she still couldn't buy that theory. True, he'd always come across as attention seeking to her and a bit egotistical, but a murderer?

Doubtful.

Maybe her stalker was lying low and had yet to come out of the woodwork.

She swallowed. That theory didn't bring much comfort, either.

* * *

Just past eleven o'clock, Kylie climbed out of her friend Taylor's car and made her way up the driveway to Steven's house. She was pleasantly rested and relaxed. The evening had flown by in a whirl of conversation—idle talk about friends, Sunday school, even the latest red-dot sale at Trestle's Department Store.

No mention of murderers, stalkers or Nick Bentley. A perfect evening.

As she entered through the front door, silence greeted her. Either Nick hadn't gotten home yet or he'd taken her advice and not waited up.

After a single step, a light snore rose, sending a band of butterflies flittering inside her stomach. Her question answered.

She slid through the foyer without a sound. The lamp from the side table in the living room illuminated softly. Kylie's instincts told her to walk quickly to her room, but she couldn't help but halt briefly beside the sofa where Nick slept.

A circle of yellow lamplight spilled over him.

Feeling quite breathless, Kylie took in Nick's sturdy physique. A Goliath of a man, he dwarfed the oversize sofa. One of his legs draped over the edge and the other stretched across the length of the couch with his foot jutting over the rolled armrest.

He looked so relaxed and peaceful. Hardly like a man battling demons. Or if Dave's assumption was correct, a man planning to kill her.

She sighed and then her heart lurched when another gentle snore escaped Nick.

Splaying a hand to her chest, she breathed deep, willing her heart to slow.

Funny, the night before, Nick had stood in the kitchen, gazed into her eyes and told her he cared about her. Now barely twenty-four hours later and only a dozen steps from where he'd said those precious words, she was staring at him and wondering if he was her stalker.

Life stank sometimes.

A single tear trailed down her cheek. She wiped it away. She almost wished the killer would call, just to touch base and let her know he was still out there. Then she'd be sure.

As she willed her phone to ring, more tears filled her eyes. Moments passed, hope shattered. Of course that wasn't going to happen. Nothing was that easy.

For now she'd keep memories of Nick close to her heart. She would not let her fears keep her from remembering him any other way.

The light of the lamp flickered, signaling her to stop musing and move on.

With her head held high, she walked out into the hallway toward her room, the path in front of her blurred as her tears continued, but she kept going. Tomorrow would be a new day. And no matter what, she would be a survivor.

* * *

Up at sunrise, Nick tightened the last bolt on the rim of the motorcycle tire. Maneuvering around town on a mode of transportation with only two wheels and a storage pouch might be somewhat limiting, but he'd be glad to have the bike working again.

He was getting vibes from Kylie that she wanted some space. Last night proved that.

A complicated situation, especially since the reason he hung around was to protect her.

Nick tossed the screwdriver and ratchet into a toolbox and got to his feet. He wiped grease off his hands with an old rag, then stuffed it in his pocket. He was beginning to feel like a regular motorcycle jock.

Although he envisioned a four-wheel-drive pickup in his future. He might even take Steven shopping with him.

The screen door slammed. Turning, he saw Kylie walk out of the house. She was dressed for work in a black skirt, medium-high heels and a teal sweater.

She looked great. He drew in a breath and released it slowly. A little more time apart might benefit him also.

"You fixed the tire." Kylie's eyes widened as she came closer.

"Yep. Up and running." He fished her keys out of his pocket and pressed them into her hand. "I appreciate the use of your car. Now it's all yours again."

A rosy-pink flushed her cheeks. "I hope you didn't feel like I was rushing you."

"Nope. I had some time. Now the cycle is ready to ride again."

She lifted her eyes to his. "I hope your evening went well last night." Her voice sounded cheery, making him wonder what kind of night she'd had.

A hot date, a new beau in her life? Was new love in the air?

Suddenly he was hot.

Just before he'd dozed off to sleep, the digital display on his phone had showed almost eleven. A late night for someone who worked the next day. Although if she'd lost any winks, it didn't show.

Squaring his shoulders, he stopped analyzing. He hated when he got ahead of himself.

"It was a good night. Got the stock put up and the store organized. How about you?"

Her head bobbed. "Very nice and relaxing."

*Relaxing?* A stalker was on the loose. Her life was in danger and she was relaxed?

"By the way," he said, "do you mind telling me who you went out to dinner with? Not that I'm being nosy. I should have asked you last night. I want to keep track of everyone you spend time with." Okay, he was rambling.

"Taylor Albright."

*Taylor.* His heart slipped, but he recovered swiftly.

"And you know him from church?"

"Her. And yes. We are in the same Sunday school."

"Taylor is a female?"

"Correct."

Sometimes it paid to be wrong. A smile tugged at the corner of his lips. He couldn't help it.

The trill of Kylie's cell phone made her jump. She dug in her purse and pulled it out. "Hello," she mumbled as she placed it to her ear.

A moment passed. Kylie's eyes went wide, then she gasped.

Nick stood still watching her. The timing was about right for the predator's next call. The creep would definitely want the world to know that he had been involved in the shoot-out in the basement of the *Asheville Daily News*.

"Wonderful. Thank you. I'll be right there." Kylie disconnected and clutched the phone to her chest.

Nick lifted a brow.

Kylie blinked up to him. "They found him."

"They found…the killer?"

She bobbled her head and the green in her eyes shimmered like diamonds.

This day was definitely heading in a better direction.

They arrived at the morgue. Nick rang the bell and they waited to be buzzed in.

"I've never been to a morgue before," Kylie whispered.

Nick had been in too many. Mostly makeshift shelters on the outskirts of the battle zones. Leaning in, he matched her tone. "You don't have to whisper. This isn't a funeral home."

She nodded and smiled, relief evident on her face. "Okay. I'm just nervous."

"You'll do fine." He'd hold off on his own feelings of relief for the moment. He still wanted to hear the full details of the story.

A technician led them down a long corridor. Gently, he gripped Kylie's elbow as he walked beside her.

They stopped at a window. Drapes drawn. Dave was already there.

"Are you ready?" The toneless cadence of Dave's voice, more empty than usual, told Nick the man had been up awhile. This case was taking its toll on everyone.

"Yes," Kylie breathed.

Nick stood close to her, his arm on her shoulder.

Dave nodded to someone behind him and the draperies slid open, exposing a glass window— the only thing that separated them from the dreary tiled room on the other side. Against the far wall, gurneys were lined up, all empty save one. The body was covered in a sheet.

Kylie pressed even closer to him. The unsure glance she sent him made him glad he was there.

With any luck this nightmare would soon be behind her. Before he could whisper that in her ear, Dave spoke up.

"Okay. Here's an update on the latest developments. The supervisor from Asheville Regional Hospital called about four this morning. She stated EMS brought in a barely conscious man, a suspected overdose. He was found slumped over the steering wheel of his car on the side of the road. By the time the paramedics got him to the ER, he was close to death. They called a code blue, but couldn't save him. As the nurses searched his belongings for an ID they found some items in his possession that concerned them. A couple of our officers went to investigate."

Dave picked up a clear plastic evidence bag off the floor. He opened it, took out a small duffel and placed it on a wooden table beside the window. Next he unzipped the duffel and pulled out a thick black portfolio and a cheap vinyl wallet, then laid them both on the table.

"These are the items recovered from the hospital." Dave picked up the file and started to take off the rubber band.

With Kylie so close, Nick could feel her quickened intake and exhale of each breath. He fastened his arm a little tighter around her shoulders, hoping to calm her some.

She stayed right by his side, with her hand on her heart. "Has this evidence already been dusted for fingerprints?" she asked, a small tremor in her voice.

Dave snapped the rubber band off the file. He glanced at Kylie, his eyes narrowed. "Every finger in the E.R. has already been through this stuff."

Case closed on that idea. Nick figured that much.

Dave opened the portfolio and as he exposed the contents inside, Kylie's gasp echoed off the cold gray walls around them.

Using quick reflexes, Nick caught her by the shoulders before she wilted to the floor.

"I can't believe this." Kylie kept repeating, shaking her head.

"They match the clippings we found in the barn, with the addition of a few recent ones," Dave said. Poking his fingers through the pile, he tugged one out for Kylie to see and then added, "There are also a dozen or so photos of the murder victims. Rather grotesque. You may not want to see those."

Kylie wagged her head. "No, that's okay. I believe you."

Nick sucked in a breath. The guy's timeline was quite unnerving. He'd missed nothing in Kylie's life. Even in the midst of the investigation, he never strayed far. Nick slid his gaze to the sheet-covered gurney behind the glass. He hoped that was the guy and not another one of the killer's victims with planted evidence.

"Dave, what showed up in the man's wallet?"

His voice turned a little gruffer than intended, but impatience egged him on.

"Not much," Dave said, scratching beside his nose. "No identification. Only a package of tobacco rolling papers and more pictures of Kylie."

Kylie glanced up at Nick, a distraught crease between her eyebrows. "I think I'm going to be sick."

"Just take a calm breath. Deep inhale and breathe it out slowly." Nick rubbed her back. "Now try to relax and when you're ready we'll take a look and see if you know this guy."

She did what he asked. After several breaths, she nodded. "Okay. I think I'm ready."

Nick and Kylie edged closer to the window. A woman wearing a mask, surgical gown and gloves rolled the gurney up to the glass. She glanced at Dave and at his nod she pulled back the top of the sheet.

No one spoke. A stony silence hung in the air.

Nick looked at the man's face. Mid-to late-twenties. Shaved head. He had scraggly facial hair and a silver-dollar-size birthmark on the side of his face, below his left cheekbone.

He looked familiar, but Nick couldn't place him. Scratching his temple, he tried to recall a name or a place that might help him pinpoint the man's identity.

He glanced at Kylie. "Do you recognize him?"

She took a deep, quavering breath and nodded as color drained from her face. "Yes. You and

Dave should remember him, too." She nodded at Nick, then glanced over at Dave. "Todd Pruitt. He was part of our high-school class. And several years ago he briefly worked as a groundskeeper at the newspaper."

"Todd Pruitt?" Dave canted his head, staring at the man. "Yes, I believe you're right."

Nick glared at the corpse again. Scars and pockmarks riddled the man's face. The bridge of his nose was crooked—he'd been in a few fights. The resemblance was vague. Todd had had long hair and smooth skin in high school, but the birthmark, a port-wine stain, hadn't changed.

"He hung out with the party crowd," Dave put in. "I remember him being loud and even gruff. Suspended several times and almost didn't graduate."

"Good memory, Dave." Nick hadn't given high school much thought over the years and details like that eluded him. That was, if he'd ever known them in the first place. One thing he did recall was that Todd had definitely hung with a different crowd then he and Kylie did. It just seemed odd that he had become obsessed with her.

"Do either of you remember if Pruitt attended the senior camp?" Nick's gaze swung between Dave and Kylie.

Biting her lip, Kylie gave a shrug. "I honestly don't recall."

"Yes. He did," Dave stated firmly, as if pounding the last nail into the coffin.

"Then again," Nick said, "this could be the work of the perpetrator. Another victim, more planted evidence?"

Dave's face hardened. He crossed his arms as if to say this was *his* investigation. "We've looked over the leads we have, and everyone involved in the investigation agrees this evidence looks promising."

*Promising* was one thing, but conclusive was what they needed. Nick held his tongue. He would chalk up Dave's attitude to fatigue and frustration. This was a big case with little clues. Solving it seemed dauntless. Now that they'd had evidence dropped into their laps, they'd need to decide if it was a lucky break or a distraction.

Nick hated to be critical, so for now he'd let Dave and his men do their job. No judgment rendered for the moment. But he'd be on high alert until he knew beyond a shadow of a doubt that Todd Pruitt was Kylie's stalker.

# SIXTEEN

Days passed and things around Asheville got quiet.

Still, something didn't feel right.

Just after dawn, Nick kicked back in a living-room chair and anchored the heel of his boot to the coffee table. He'd been up for hours.

He'd crashed early the night before, dead tired by the time his body hit the memory-foam mattress in his little apartment. He should have slept great, especially after his cramped sleeping quarters over the past week. But instead of sleeping, he'd tossed and turned.

By four o'clock he finally gave up, climbed out of bed and sank into the old recliner by the window. He glanced at Steven's house next door. The lights were out. Hopefully, Kylie was able to sleep.

Nick's jaw clenched. He still couldn't get the murder investigation off his mind. And the more he thought about it, the more doubts he had.

Ever since the discovery of Todd Pruitt's body, he'd been mulling over the quandary in his head. He'd been convinced that the investigation would continue. There were too many holes yet to be filled. But that wasn't happening.

Last night, just before nine, Dave had called to

notify Kylie that they had sufficient evidence to link Pruitt to the two most recent murders. And although Conrad's murder remained unsolved, his case was being reopened with Pruitt as the main suspect.

The Asheville Stalker case had officially been closed.

Tied up with a nice little bow. The evidence tucked safely in a bag, the perpetrator dead.

No one left to question. No lingering clues.

The police obviously wanted the case behind them. Wanted a good night's sleep.

Nick now had insomnia.

Folding his arms across his chest, he thought back to the beginning of the whole ordeal and sifted through the facts as he knew them.

The airport murder had come out of nowhere. No advance warning. Only a phone call from the killer to herald his first victim and to establish himself as the murderer. Then Kylie's elevator ride and the scavenger hunt to Jake Plyler's barn. More phone calls. A note. Another murder victim. The basement incident.

The killer's crimes had made headlines. He invoked fear in people, had them looking over their shoulders. Especially Kylie, the person he stalked.

A psychopath's dream.

Nick flopped his head against the recliner cushion and scrubbed a hand over his face.

A perfectly orchestrated crime by an obsessed mind. Not a mind riddled with drugs.

Like Todd Pruitt's.

Toxicology results showed polysubstance—the guy had more types of drugs in his system than a hospital pharmacy, and alcohol to boot.

This wasn't a first for Pruitt. A habit. An addiction. Nobody started off using drugs like that.

In the army, Nick and his men had hunted down their share of murderers, terrorists, even a crazed stalker or two. He'd learned early on that criminals were crafty, even brilliant, their crimes complicated.

Admittedly, some crimes were easier to solve than others. But to find all the supporting evidence in the suspect's possession, carried around in a little bag? Not happening.

Too convenient and clean.

Pruitt might have been hired help, but no way was he the instigator.

Nick bit back a groan.

The killer was still out there. Idly watching. Idly waiting for the right time to strike again. He could feel it.

Maybe even working among the detectives or media, somehow related to the investigation.

Nick hated to be suspicious, discount the police detectives' capability or rationale. But even more so, he couldn't discount his gut.

The worst part was, Kylie probably wouldn't

buy in to his suspicions. She was too hyped up about getting back to her life.

And the past few days had been awkward between them. Kylie acted a little more distant and he reciprocated, giving her space. He understood where she was coming from.

The truth of matter—he'd be leaving soon. A goodbye was inevitable.

Hard on both of them, but soon they'd be consumed with their own lives again.

Logical. Too bad the heart didn't really know logic.

Kylie wrestled with the bulging suitcase on the bed and tried to zip it shut. Packed to the gills. It hadn't seemed so difficult to close when she'd packed the first time. But wasn't that how things went? What once fit together perfectly no longer fit the same once it was disrupted.

And that truth ran the gamut.

Articles in a suitcase. Packaging in a box. A relationship. Her and Nick.

Suppressing a sigh, Kylie pressed down, adding more weight, and managed to tug the zipper around the black bag.

Okay. She got to her feet and brushed off her hands. Time to get going.

She yanked up the roller handle and walked out of the room.

Nick was sitting on the sofa in the living room,

a vacant look on his face, his eyes heavy lidded. He looked so peaceful. So handsome. How could she have considered for a moment that he might be her stalker?

Shaking her head, Kylie took a step into the family room and then stopped. She looked closely, but couldn't decide if Nick was half-asleep or deep in thought.

Maybe he was reordering his thoughts, convincing himself that the past was the past. And that the feelings he'd once felt for her needed to be explored again.

*Stop it.* Kylie pushed off the dream. The near kiss in the kitchen had only been a fleeting moment of emotion for him. He was well past it now. Nick had big plans for his future that didn't involve her.

With a slow exhale, she changed her way of thinking. She would not succumb to fantasy any longer.

Crazy that she'd even allowed her thoughts to drift, considering the ache it caused. What had started out as a small twinge in her chest the moment she laid eyes on Nick at the airport had progressed into a painful spasm when she thought about him leaving again.

Instinctively she pressed two fingers to her chest. A bruised heart, she knew from experience, took a long time to heal.

She cleared her throat.

Nick looked up from the sofa. A smile chased away his impassive expression. "Good morning."

"Good morning." She matched his smile. "I hope I didn't disrupt your nap."

"No. I wasn't sleeping." He got to his feet and stretched his back. "I've been up for hours, sitting around mulling over the facts of the case. I got here a little while ago. What about you? You're up pretty early."

"I have to get to my house to drop off my things before I go into work."

Nick glanced past her to the bags in the hallway behind her. Then he flashed Kylie a puzzled look. "You're leaving already?"

The question surprised her. The case was closed. Why wouldn't she leave?

She nodded her reply.

"I'm not sure you should leave yet."

An awful coldness seeped through her as she searched his gaze. Was he trying to play with her emotions? "Why shouldn't I leave?"

"There are a few things about the case and the investigation that concern me."

"The case is closed."

"I understand that. However, I have my concerns that Dave and his men made a premature decision."

"Meaning?"

"Why don't you sit down?" He gestured toward the sofa.

Kylie shook her head. "I'll stand." She didn't like the way the conversation was heading. She didn't want doubts in Nick's head. She wanted his investigative mind to concur with the police.

"I'm not a hundred percent sure that Todd Pruitt is the killer. I've been digging around in his past and I don't have a good feeling about him being the one."

Kylie's pulse started to race. "Is anyone ever a hundred percent sure of anything?"

"Everyone should be when it comes to murder."

Kylie bristled at that. "I feel okay about this. I think the investigation was conclusive, and I believe Todd is the killer."

"The guy was a drug addict. Do you really think he would be capable enough to commit such calculated crimes?"

"I didn't know Todd well enough to have an opinion of what he would be capable of. But I do know what he had in his possession at the time of his death."

"Okay, consider this. Why would he be carrying around the evidence?"

"Nick, you said it yourself, guys like this are obsessed. And their motives don't have to make sense."

"Although serial killers have skewed thoughts, their minds are sharp." Before she could comment, Nick held up his hand. "Did Todd ever ask you out? In high school or after?"

Without hesitation Kylie shook her head.

"At any time did he ever flirt or hint around that he might be interested in you?"

"No. I never spoke more than two words to the guy. Including in high school."

"Okay. I'm not saying he doesn't have some part in this, but I don't see him as your stalker."

"Nick. Please."

Nick plowed a hand through his hair. "Kylie, I have a gut feeling that this guy isn't the one. You need to trust me on this."

Trust? As if that was easy. She couldn't even trust her own heart these days.

And spending more time with this man wouldn't be good for her. Sending him a sidelong glance, she found his russet-brown eyes fastened on her.

She breathed deep. Things could only get worse.

"Nick, I can't keep living in the shadows. I need to get my life back on track."

"I understand. I just wish you'd lie low for another few days."

"I have a friend who is willing to stay with me for a few days. Two sets of instincts are better than one." She tried for a smile but it was a bust.

A dark brow lifted. "And who is this friend?"

She squared her shoulders. This was worse than trying to convince her father that backpacking through Mexico with some of her college friends was perfectly safe. He'd never bought it. She never went.

But she was older now and Nick was not her father. "Julie Masters. She's in my Sunday school class."

"If you're going to have someone stay with you, you might as well stay here."

Still a little unnerved about everything that had happened over the past few weeks, she almost considered it. But one look into Nick's pleading eyes and her heart was a goner.

Staying would only prolong the agony already building in her chest.

"I've been enough of a burden. I'm ready to leave." Before she could betray any other emotion, she picked up her smallest bag.

He stood there a moment, hands stuffed awkwardly in his pockets. She knew that look. Insistent. Persuasive. She didn't blink. She wasn't going to budge.

"Okay." He finally nodded. "But know you're always welcome here. Don't hesitate to call me if something comes up." He didn't look completely happy, but neither was she.

Nick paused a moment and then walked toward her, holding out his hand. "Let me help you with your bags."

He wasn't about to beg her to stay. Not easily persuaded, she'd need proof. And he'd get her that proof.

Ten minutes later, he slammed the trunk of her

car. "Is there anything else you need me to get from the house?"

She shook her head. "I have everything. And I want to thank you for all you've done. Words can't express my gratitude."

He held up a hand. "Don't be too thankful yet. Let's make sure this thing is really over."

"Nick." She averted her gaze.

"I'm not trying to be a spoiler. I'm just not convinced."

Instead of expressing annoyance, she smiled. "With Steven coming home soon, where will you go from here?"

Subject changed. He let it go. Maybe they did need to shift gears.

He gave it a few seconds, then answered, "I still have some things to finish around here." Nick leaned against her car and crossed his arms, frustrated that she couldn't seem to understand.

"Again, Nick, thanks for everything. I better get going." She gestured to the driver's-side door that he rested against.

Nick straightened and opened the door for her.

He was tempted to hug her, but stopped himself. Apparently Kylie felt the same way, because she breezed by him and climbed into the car.

Another awkward moment with Kylie Harper and he took full blame.

Kylie blinked up at him through the open door.

"If I don't happen to see you again before you leave, I hope your plans turn out well."

This was a small town. He was still investigating the murders. She'd see him again.

And he was okay with that.

Before Kylie could pull the door shut, he leaned in. "It's been a tough few weeks, but aside from that, I enjoyed seeing you again."

Kylie blinked, then a hint of a smile touched her lips. She didn't respond, but the sudden glint in her eyes gave him pause.

"I mean every word," he said as he captured her fingers. Bringing her hand to his lips, he brushed a kiss across her knuckles.

Kylie cried nearly all the way home.

How dare Nick mess with her emotions like that? He had no intention of pursuing anything with her, yet the mixed signals she was getting from him had her heart ready to burst.

She didn't blame Nick. The culprit was her delusional thoughts.

A mind was a funny thing. From the get-go Nick had let her know his plans, none of which included her. Yet her heart continued to override logic. *He loves me, he loves me not* swung in her head like a possessed pendulum. Delusional.

Gritting her teeth, Kylie gripped the steering wheel and maneuvered down the dirt road that led to her house.

She'd had enough. Her heart was bruised and battered. With a sniffle, she vowed to push past this season in her life. Once and for all she'd forget about Nick.

Not because she didn't love him, but because she could never have him.

Rejection was a terrible thing. Even after ten years it didn't get better. In fact, it was worse.

Sighing, she parked in the driveway, not bothering to pull into the garage. She only needed to drop off her bags.

On her way out the door, she paused in the foyer. She inhaled and pulled in the lingering scent of aged wood, fresh paint and vanilla potpourri. Home.

She felt better.

When she arrived at the newspaper office, the buzz of excitement about the capture and subsequent death of the serial killer flitted around her. Max, on the other hand, she was told by one of her colleagues, was a little down in the mouth.

Poor thing. His fast track to stardom was now a bust.

Three hours into her day and she still hadn't seen her boss. Busy in his office or sulking? It didn't matter. Her life was getting back to normal.

"Kylie, there's a call for you on line four," the sports editor hollered from across the room.

Kylie punched four and picked up the phone.

It was Max. She fought not to cringe.

"I'd like to meet with you in my office in thirty minutes."

Kylie peered at her watch. She should have taken her break earlier. So much for lunch. "All right. See you in thirty."

When Kylie arrived at Max's office, he was waiting.

"Take a seat, Kylie." He gestured to one of the chairs on the opposite side of his desk.

Kylie settled into the blue armchair and crossed her legs. She had no idea why Max had asked her there and he didn't seem to be in a hurry to tell her.

She lifted her gaze to him. He had his palms pressed together, his index fingers resting against his lips. Deep in thought. This didn't look good.

A moment later Dave walked in. He took the seat next to her.

She glanced between the two men. If bad news was brewing, she hoped it didn't involve her. But with the vibes she was getting, fat chance.

Dave spoke up first. "Kylie, I have a few concerns about the investigation. I asked Max to be here because of the incident that took place in the building. I'd like to keep him in the loop so he can keep an eye out for anything suspicious."

"Wait a minute." Kylie scooted forward in her seat, now perched on the edge. "You told me yesterday that the case had been closed. That evidence concluded Todd Pruitt was the stalker and responsible for the two recent homicides. Maybe even Conrad's murder."

Dave gave a slow nod. "Both of those facts are correct. But now we're looking into a possible accomplice."

"Well, how about that," Max said, a slow grin cracking his lips.

Kylie plopped back in the chair. She had a sinking feeling. Maybe they had closed the case too soon. Nick was right. "What changed, Dave?"

"Pruitt got out of prison earlier this year after serving four years for breaking and entering and assault with a deadly weapon."

"Sounds like the perfect candidate for the crime."

"Except some of the pictures and articles in his possession were from the time he was in prison."

"Oh." She sank back in the chair.

"We've just started our investigation," Dave continued. "Are you aware that Nick is digging around for information on his own?"

A shrug from Kylie. "I know he has some of the same concerns as you. He didn't mention an accomplice, but he has reservations about Todd. He doesn't think he fits the serial-killer profile."

"What is this guy, a criminal psychiatrist, too?" Max butted in.

Kylie raised a hand. "Nick's had significant

training as a Delta Force officer, including criminal psychology."

"He's a trained killer with a razor-sharp mind, that's what he is."

That comment brought Kylie's eyes back to Dave. "What are you getting at?"

He gave her a chilly look and inclined his head. "Nick is correct about one thing—Todd doesn't fit the profile. He wasn't that smart, but Nick Bentley is."

That brought Kylie to her feet. "That's absurd. Why would he be digging around for evidence on himself?"

Dave didn't hesitate. "To cover his tracks. Maybe Pruitt died sooner than he planned."

Kylie planted her hands on her hips. "Or maybe Pruitt wasn't the killer at all. Maybe he was another victim and the evidence was planted."

Dave stared after her for a long moment and then stood. "Nick's theory, I'm sure. You can believe whatever you like, Kylie. But either way, be careful. Your life is still in danger."

*Your life is still in danger.* The words reached inside her like a fist clenching her heart and sent cold chills twining through her.

Kylie pressed a hand to her chest, working to stay calm. She'd had enough looking over her shoulder. Enough living in the past.

With a heavy sigh, she lifted a prayer. *Father,*

*God, please protect me. And give me the wisdom
I need to get through this.*

Her next breath brought a morsel of calm.

"I'll be careful," she said, her gaze trailing back
to Dave. "But I'd like you to rethink your theory
on Nick. The four years Pruitt was in prison, Nick
was fighting in the Middle East."

Dave shrugged, his stare unflinching. "Nick
lives in an undercover world. He can get his hands
on whatever information he wants."

For a fleeting moment, scenarios whipped
through Kylie's mind like a tornado. As quickly,
she pushed through the confusion clouding her
heart. It couldn't be Nick.

"Wait a minute." Max held up a hand. "Correct
me if I'm wrong, but wasn't someone shooting at
Bentley in this very building? Dave, do you think
it was Pruitt?"

"We haven't gotten that far. No one saw a
shooter. For all we know it could have been Nick
in there alone." A little sharpness crept into Dave's
voice.

"Wow. This is some newsworthy stuff." Max's
face brightened.

"No," Dave snapped. "As far as the public is
concerned, this case is closed until we have some
solid evidence."

Max jumped to his feet. "Detective, come on.
If you have information suggesting that there's
still a killer out there, it's our duty to let the public

know. Not just because it's newsworthy information, but because the citizens of Asheville have a right to protect themselves."

Kylie ran her fingers through her hair, letting Max plead and lecture another moment before she interrupted. "Max, just an FYI. The only evidence Detective Michelson has on Nick at the moment is a gut feeling. Isn't that right, Dave?"

Dave's face lost all color. He cleared his voice. "Like I said, we're still investigating."

Until they had something conclusive, she didn't want to hear about his speculations. If she had to trust anybody's gut feeling, it would be Nick's.

"Kylie, understand something." Dave's voice fell into a less professional beat. "I'm not trying to pin anything on Nick. I'm just being proactive."

She nodded. Dave had a job to do, she understood that. "I understand, Dave. I don't want anyone falsely accused. But if the killer is still out there, I'd like you to find him."

"And don't forget we have first dibs on the story," Max interjected.

Dave pulled a disgusted face. He crossed the room in three long strides and walked out the door.

Rubbing his head, Max sank into his leather desk chair, looking deflated. He zeroed in his languid gaze on Kylie. "You don't buy the detective's theory about Nick?"

Kylie hesitated. Took a breath. "No."

"Too bad. It sounded like a good one. A story that would sell papers."

Without commenting, Kylie shook her head and followed in Dave's footsteps, out the door and back to her desk.

# SEVENTEEN

"Take it easy, Steven. Don't try to move too quickly." Nick kept a protective hand on his brother's back as he maneuvered his walker over the wooden threshold going into the kitchen.

"I think I like the crutches better," Steven groaned. "Bearing weight on this leg is killing me."

"No pain, no gain, bro," Nick said, pulling a chair from the table and positioning it behind his brother. "Ease down into this."

Steven loosened his iron-man grip on the walker and dropped into the wooden chair. Right then and there Nick knew he wouldn't be going anywhere anytime soon.

"Just getting around the house was a lot harder than I expected." Steven propped his foot on an adjacent chair.

"Sorry. I guess I don't have the Nurse Nadine touch." Nick smiled and set a glass of tea on the table for Steven.

"Thanks." Steven picked up the glass. "By the way, my private nurse will be stopping by in a little while." He waggled his eyebrows.

"Was that a not-so-subtle hint for me to take a hike when she shows up?" Nick settled in a chair at the table.

"Uh, yeah." Steven smiled and took a swig.

Nick laughed. "I guess it's back to the apartment for me."

Steven shrugged. He swirled his glass, the ice clinking. "I have a better idea. Why don't you check in with Kylie? I haven't heard you talk about her the last few days."

*Why don't you mind your own business?* Nick breathed deep. "Actually, I haven't seen or talked to her since she left last week."

"Ouch. Not going well, huh?"

Nick crossed his arms. "I haven't had a reason to contact her. Dave hasn't been as forthcoming with information about Pruitt, and I've been hitting brick walls trying to dig around on my own. And she must not have gotten any phone calls from her stalker, because she hasn't contacted me, either."

"Why do you need a reason? Just call her up for a date."

"It's not like that. We're only friends. I'm just trying to help her out."

What started off as a chuckle from Steven quickly bumped up to a laugh. "Nick, who are you trying to fool? You love that girl, you always have."

"And what do you know about love, little brother? You have a new girl every week."

"I know enough to recognize that I've never felt the same way about any woman as you feel about

Kylie. It is evident by the way you talk about her. The look in your eye, the tone of your voice."

Nick rocked back in his chair. He hadn't expected this. "I'm concerned about her as a friend, that's all."

"You love her, man. Ten years and it's still there."

This from a man who didn't know how to focus while riding a bike, let alone focus on a long-term relationship. "And when did you take up counseling for a hobby?"

"It doesn't take a PhD to figure you out."

Nick opened his mouth. Shut it again. Frowned. "We're just friends. Period. We've both changed and moved on in our lives."

"Uh, maybe you've changed, but moving on, I don't buy it."

Nick just shook his head.

"Look at you. You haven't had a serious relationship since you and Kylie broke up," Steven reminded him. "And why do you think Kylie's still single? She's waiting for you, man. Waiting for her soldier in shining armor to come back."

Nick rolled his eyes. "I doubt that's true. I think that's your brain injury talking."

"Nope. Scan came back negative." Amusement underscored his brother's words. "No signs of a concussion." He tapped the side of his head.

*Or a brain.* Nick smiled inside.

"You love her?"

Nick glanced at his brother, a knowing look

in his eye. "Enough questions, okay? Kylie and I are friends."

"Friends now, but who knows about the future? Stick around and see if anything transpires. Besides, I wouldn't mind having a brother around."

"Sorry, Asheville isn't the place for me."

"Sure it is. We can use you around here. You can run for police commissioner or be an investigator. You're finding out the P.D. is undertrained in that area."

Nick wagged his head. "I'm not cut out for that."

"What are you cut out for, Nick? Running from the past?"

His chest stung with that comment. But Nick ignored it and leaned forward, propping his elbows on the table. "Even trying to acquire public information about Pruitt is difficult. I might have to enlist help from some buddies of mine."

"Smooth, brother." Steven gestured with his glass. "The way you just switched subjects there. But I'll let you be for now."

"Thank you." Nick grinned.

"So what have you found on Pruitt so far?"

"Let's see." Nick linked his hands behind his head. "Besides spending four years in the pen, he's been in and out of rehab for years. At the time of his death he had an active bench warrant out for two DUIs and over the years he hasn't held a job longer than seven months."

"Model citizen." Steven moaned a little as he shifted in his chair.

"And somehow he's been deemed smart enough to stay hidden from law enforcement while committing gruesome murders." Nick sat up. "How about an ice pack?"

"I was going to wait for Nadine, but if you wouldn't mind."

"Not a problem." Nick went to the refrigerator and filled a ziplock bag with ice. "The more I find out about Pruitt, the more I'm sure he died by the hand of the predator and the killer is still out there."

"So how are you going to prove it?"

"Not sure. There hasn't been a mumble from the killer since Pruitt's overdose. And Pruitt is the only suspect in the case. He had the right evidence in his possession, planted or not, and was living in Asheville when the two recent murders occurred. And if Detective Dave is correct, Pruitt was also at Camp Golden Rock with us. Conrad's case is now being reopened with Pruitt as the main suspect."

Nick draped a dish towel around the bag of ice and handed it to Steven.

"Are you sure Pruitt went to your senior camp? I didn't think he even graduated high school." Steven plopped the ice bag on his elevated knee, giving Nick a puzzled glance. "If I remember right, he'd been expelled earlier in the year. Fireworks in one of the toilets in the boys' bathroom or something like that. It was big news at the time."

Vaguely Nick recalled the story. Then it hit him. "Is my yearbook around here somewhere?"

"Mom left a couple of your boxes. They're in the basement."

Nick found the cardboard box right away. His mom had been good at labeling everything. He brushed off the top and started sifting through old jerseys, varsity letters, report cards, even a manila folder of pictures he didn't bother opening. More photos of him and Kylie. Memories he didn't need roused at the moment.

Four stacked yearbooks filled the bottom of the box. He pulled out the one from his senior year. Turning to the index, he quickly scanned the page, stopping at *senior class photo*. He flipped to page eighty-three. On the top half of the page, a black-and-white picture featured over a hundred and fifty senior students huddled together for a senior class shot. It had been taken the first day of the second semester.

Nick skimmed over the faces, pausing on Kylie. Her smile lit up the page. He took a deep breath and moved along, stopping again when he came to Conrad. A full-toothed grin creased his face. He looked so happy. So much alive. Nick closed his eyes and pictured Conrad sprawled across the deck, lying in blood, a slit across his neck.

A wave of nausea rolled over him. He pulled in

a steady breath and moved along, down the rows of smiling faces. When he got to the last picture, he shook his head in relief. Pruitt wasn't among them.

Now more than ever he believed that Pruitt wasn't the stalker or the killer.

"Hey. Nice flowers."

The deep baritone voice coming from directly behind her blasted through Kylie's nervous system like a bullet. Gripping the spade she'd been digging with, she jumped up and whirled around to find Nick with his hands in his pockets and glaring at her.

"Nick, I asked you to not to sneak up on me like that."

"Sorry. I thought you would have heard me walking up the driveway." He smiled at her, his tone pleasant and not at all threatening. Well, except for the fact that he was dangerously attractive. A hazard to her well-being. Especially since it had taken the past week to finally get him out of her head.

She dropped the spade and pulled earbuds from her ears, leaving them to dangle at her neck.

He lifted a dark brow at her. "That explains why you didn't hear me. I purposely tried to put a little punch in my step."

"I appreciate that. But the music drowns out the

distant noise." And helped keep her thoughts clear and not focused on one certain old boyfriend.

"That could cost you."

The affectionate scolding in his eyes brought a lump to her throat. She shrugged. "You're right. But on a positive note, my friend Julie has been staying with me every night after she gets off work."

"That's better than nothing." A tentative smile again.

"And everything has been quiet. No phone calls. No hint of a perpetrator."

He shifted his weight and didn't respond. But he had that *not yet* look in his eyes.

She swallowed. Hopefully, Dave wasn't right about Nick. Immediately she reined that thought in. The only danger Nick posed was to her heart. Which at the moment hammered double time in her chest.

She looked past him and down the driveway. "How'd you get here?"

"Steven's motorcycle. I bit dust the whole way. No way was I tackling that dirt road."

She wanted to laugh. But instead she said, "I wish you had called before you came."

"Why? So you could arrange not to be here?"

Her gaze snapped back to his and those dark eyes seemed to stare right into her heart. He knew what she was thinking. Of course he did.

"I've left you several voice mails."

She shrugged. "I had a lot of work to catch up on. I haven't had a chance to call you back. I assumed if it was urgent you would have said so in your message." Forcing her gaze from his, she brushed potting soil from her hands, feigning nonchalance. "So how are you coming with the investigation on Pruitt?"

Hopefully, Nick would get the hint that she didn't want to explain why she'd been avoiding his calls.

"I've learned a few things."

She pushed hair from her face. "Well, before you drop any bombshells on me, would you like something to drink?"

Eyebrows lifted, he nodded. "Actually, I would. It's quite a hike up that hill from the highway. I wouldn't mind something cold."

"Okay." She gestured to the white wooden rocking chairs on the porch. "Make yourself at home. I'll be back in a moment."

She headed into the house and Nick trailed in behind her. She'd expected him to wait on the porch; apparently he hadn't taken the hint.

Leaving him in the family room, she strode into the kitchen. She fetched two glasses from the cabinet and filled them with iced tea.

"The view is really nice, just like I remember." His voice carried in from the other room.

Kylie added three teaspoons of sugar to one glass. The way Nick liked his. She gave a quick stir and then walked into the family room. Nick's back was to her. He was staring out the large picture window at the mountain range in the distance.

"It is beautiful. That's why I love it here."

He turned around and crossed his arms, his sturdy frame draped against the window ledge. "And why you love Asheville?"

She gave a slight shrug. "Partly. I also love the town. The people. It's home."

"What about the memories?" He spoke low, bitterness lacing his tone.

Kylie knew what he was getting at. She breathed a prayer of thanks that the memories that haunted him no longer held her hostage. Sadness would always remain in her heart, along with regret, but Nick had it so much worse than that. *Lord, help him,* she added.

She took a quick breath. "Memories don't ever abandon me. No matter where I go, they're always there."

"Ah. But they fade. They become minimized in the back of one's mind. Lost in the distraction of new chaos." He pushed away from the wall and sauntered toward her, his gaze never leaving hers.

She blinked. "Are the pleasant memories lost along with the painful ones?"

He paused, drew a finger to his lip. "I hadn't considered that, but I guess the answer would be yes. A casualty that can't be helped."

And she was his casualty. Kylie's throat nearly

closed up with emotion. She swallowed it back. "For me the pleasant memories outweigh the bad. I can still enjoy life in Asheville in spite of my mistakes, my losses."

He closed the space between them, and she handed him his tea.

Nick lifted his glass in a toast. "Here's to you, Kylie. The strongest woman I know. You make the best of life's disappointments. See the good in people. What I feel when I look around Asheville is regret and guilt."

She wanted to shake him, make him understand. He wasn't responsible for Conrad's death. She opened her mouth to remind him of that, but he picked up the conversation again.

"My one concern is that when I leave Asheville again, I'll have an even greater regret."

"Greater regret?" Kylie echoed, hoping it had something to do with her.

"Yes." He nodded and as she waited for him to expound on his comment, he lifted his glass and took a long drink.

She stared at him for several nail-biting moments, watching his Adam's apple bob in his throat. Finally he lowered his near-empty glass, licked his lips. "That was refreshing. Thank you."

"And you were saying?"

For the next few seconds he didn't speak, and when he did, his brow furrowed and his lips tensed a bit. "Kylie, I don't want anything to happen to you. I know you want this stalker business behind you, but your being out here by yourself is a concern to me. A friend coming at night doesn't protect you enough. I want you safe."

Okay. Not the revelation she'd hoped for. But the shadow in his eyes told her there was more to this story.

"This is about Todd Pruitt?"

"It's about you being safe. I'm not sure where Pruitt fits into the scheme, but he wasn't the mastermind. If he was involved, it was with the recent victims. He didn't attend the senior camp with us. An ex–Delta Force buddy of mine is a private detective and got ahold of his criminal records. It seems Pruitt was in juvenile detention at the time of the senior camping trip."

"So he wasn't there when Conrad was killed?"

"No."

"But Dave said he remembered—"

"Dave was wrong."

"I don't understand. Dave seemed so sure." Kylie's legs suddenly felt weak. She carried her drink to the closest armchair and sank into it.

"I don't think Dave tried to lead us astray. It was probably hopeful thinking on his part. Many details of that trip remain vague in my mind."

Hers also. She swallowed, holding on to a thread of hope and grasping at straws at the same time. "Maybe Conrad's murder isn't connected to the others. Maybe Pruitt was a copycat just trying to take credit. Your theory early on."

Nick shook his head. "That was before I read the recent autopsy reports and compared them to Conrad's. The cause of death listed for all three victims was strangulation. They all died before their necks were slit." Then he added, "The blade used in each instance was believed to be a small scalpel. And behind the right ear of each man was a tiny laceration in the shape of an X. It was described like a scratch in Conrad's report, and has been consistent with the other two victims."

The last shred of hope that her stalker was dead and gone fizzled and disappeared.

Kylie set down her drink and caved against the cushions. "Are we back to square one?"

Nick hesitated, then nodded. "Pretty much."

"I don't know how the police haven't figured this out. How could they have closed the case so quickly?"

"My guess is that the local detectives were overwhelmed. Pruitt came along, the evidence was there. They stopped looking for clues. Now they're reopening Conrad's case, with Pruitt as the main suspect."

"But Pruitt couldn't have been involved if he was in juvenile detention at the time of Conrad's death. Does Dave know about that?"

"Dave hasn't been very forthcoming with information. And he actually asked me to butt out of the case. His jurisdiction. I understand."

No. Nick didn't understand. Kylie swallowed. "Did you know Dave thinks Pruitt had an accomplice?"

Nick's eyes brightened. "Good. Then he's not as off track as I thought. That means they're still digging for clues."

"Nick." Kylie scooted to the edge of her seat. "Dave believes you are the accomplice."

For a second, Nick gaped, then he started to laugh. "No wonder Dave's been acting odd."

It was a truism that the closest person to the victim became a prime suspect. But it shouldn't take a reasonable detective long to dispute that theory.

"What kind of evidence do they have?"

"You were at the camp when Conrad was killed. More murders started happening when you arrived back in town. You're a trained soldier and, in his mind, capable of killing."

Nick nodded. "Contrived guesses, but not evidence."

"I suppose."

"And what do you think, Kylie? Do you think I killed Conrad? Or would ever hurt you?"

"Well, this has been such a confusing time." She ran a hand through her auburn curls and wrinkled her nose. "Everyone has been pointing fingers, suspecting one person or another. For fleeting

moments, I suppose I've considered every option."
As she circled the question cautiously, Nick's heart
plummeted like a torpedo to the pit of his stomach.

She didn't trust him. But how could she? He'd
abandoned her once. Turned his back on the
woman he'd loved.

Nick took a breath. *God, I know it's been a
while, but please help me figure this out. I still
care about Kylie. Please show me what to do,
Lord, to keep her safe. I need Your help.*

The revelation that hit Nick almost took his
breath away. All these years he'd held on to guilt,
trying to heal on his own. *Forgive me, Lord.* Emotion rose in his chest. He no longer wanted to do
life alone.

"Kylie, I know you're hearing conflicting suspicions from everyone involved in this case, but
you need to trust me on this. The serial killer is
still out there. He may be lying low now, but he
will strike again."

"Nick, please, let's not jump too quick. For all
we know the killer is back in hiding. He may have
caused enough chaos and fear to satisfy his mon-
strous desires for another ten years."

"No, Kylie, I'm not going to take that chance.
I think you need to come back to my brother's
house. You'll be safe there until the real culprit
is found."

The look in Kylie's eyes grew tender. "I appreciate your concern. If the phone calls start again

or if I start to feel unsafe, I'll come hang out at Steven's house. Until then I just want to get my life back to normal."

Normal? He didn't even know what normal was anymore. "I can't force you to do anything, but I want you to call me with any concern. And please answer when I call. I want to keep up with you."

She nodded and he smiled. He wasn't a hundred percent okay with the situation. Progress nonetheless.

From her front porch, Kylie watched Nick head down the dirt driveway to his motorcycle. She wasn't surprised by the tightening in her chest, knowing Nick would soon be out of her life forever. Still, her heart was warmed by the fact that he wanted to ensure her safety. If nothing else, she thanked God for that.

# EIGHTEEN

For the first time in years, Nick felt as though he had a direction. God had taken hold of his life.

A moment of surrender and all things seemed possible.

Nick picked up the yearbook from his brother's kitchen table. He needed to focus on two things. First, figure out who Kylie's stalker was, bring him down and get him convicted. Second, move on with his life. Start fresh. Leave the past in the past.

Daunting? No way. He was up for the challenge.

He opened the yearbook and turned to the photo of their senior class. He knew right where to go—he'd marked the page.

What he was looking for, he wasn't sure. Still, he scanned the faces, zeroed in on the eyes. Studied each student's body language, looking for clues. If one was a killer, what would stand out? He blew out a breath and then gave the photo another searching look. Nothing.

Nick set the book on the table, let the cover slam shut.

He was missing something. Something right under his nose.

Scratching his right temple, he went to the refrigerator and grabbed a canned soda. One long swig and the sweet flavor satisfied his taste buds and hopefully cranked up his brain.

Nick sank into a chair at the table and as he drummed his fingers on the wooden arm, he rolled dozens of motives around in his mind, possible perpetrators and umpteen scenarios.

Steven appeared in the doorway. He lifted the walker with ease and stepped into the room.

Nick grinned at his brother. "You're getting around better."

"I'm not as stiff as before. It's definitely getting easier to walk. I can't wait to ditch this contraption." He patted the metal frame.

"Shouldn't be long and you'll be ready to run marathons."

"Yeah. I was gearing up for the Timber's Edge bike marathon when I got hurt. I might start working toward that again."

Nick tried not cringe, but couldn't stop himself. "Steven. I'm thinking bikes aren't your best friend."

Steven glanced at the cast taking up the space between his left thigh and his ankle. "This is true."

"There's always golf."

"You remember, don't you?" Steven smiled. "I got hit with three stray balls during a golf outing in middle school."

"I guess I forgot." Nick grinned. "There's swimming. Nah. You could drown doing that."

"You've always been the athletic one. And I've just been cursed to have all the girls." Steven shook his head, feigning a sigh.

Unlike Steven, Nick had only cared about one girl. Immediately, he squashed that stray thought and swallowed. "Speaking of women, I'm still at a loss about Kylie's stalker. Although it has to be someone who went to high school with us."

"That's an unnerving thought." Steven thumped his walker across the floor and lowered himself into a chair by the table.

"Well, there's not much about this murderer that isn't unnerving." Nick opened the yearbook and started poring over the picture again.

"Hey. I almost forgot. The police were by earlier. They had some questions for you."

Nick snapped his head up and looked at his brother. "They came by to question me?"

A shrug from Steven. "I guess."

"What did you tell them?"

"I said you were working at the store today and then running errands. That is what you were doing, right?"

"Yeah." And a little personal business he wouldn't get into.

"Why? Is there something wrong?"

"Actually, the police consider me a suspect in the murders. They believe Pruitt was involved, but they also think he had an accomplice."

"What? They think you and Pruitt—" Steven leaned in, his eyes wide.

Nick nodded and started to peruse the faces again. "That's what I hear."

"I hope you set them straight."

"Nope. Haven't talked to them and don't plan to."

"Why, may I ask?"

He looked up, caught Steven's stare. "They have nothing that could link me to the murders except speculation. But if they're looking for a scapegoat, I don't want it to be me. Especially since I haven't gotten to the bottom of who the real killer is yet."

Nick straightened in his seat as a notion flashed in his mind like a beam of light. He dug his cell out of his pocket and called Kylie.

She picked right up. "Hey there."

"Hey there yourself. I just had a thought. The pictures you took when we hiked the mountain that night at camp, do you still have them?"

"Yes, why?"

"I have a hunch. Do you think you can locate them quickly?" Now that the police wanted to question him, time was really of the essence.

"I had all my photos put on disc a couple years ago. There are thousands of pictures on twelve discs, so it could take me a little time."

"You took some photos of the camp from one of the overlooks just before nightfall. Blow them up and see what you find. I'll be by shortly."

"What am I looking for?"

"Anything unusual. When you find it, you'll know."

"Okay."

On her trek to the spare bedroom, Kylie shook off a chill. She hadn't looked at the photos Nick referred to in years. And even then she'd only glimpsed them.

She entered the room, marched to the closet and pulled open the door. Small boxes and plastic tubs lined the top shelf and larger ones took up the space on the floor. She popped a hand on her hip as her gaze skittered from one container to the next. She'd been meaning to organize this stuff.

*If I were a disc, where would I be?* She huffed out a breath. Up on her toes, she reached for a cardboard box on the top shelf and started with that.

Forty minutes and five storage containers later, she pulled out a CD case with twelve discs inside. She dropped into her swivel desk chair and wiggled the mouse until the screen saver popped up. She loaded the disc labeled *High School Years*.

Sucking on the corner of her lip, Kylie sat forward and scrolled through a menagerie of photos, sweet memories drifting through her mind as she glimpsed silly pictures of her and Nick. And every glance made the love in her heart expand.

Tamping down her growing sentiment, she

continued to scan the images. Hundreds rolled by, and toward the end of the album, the first picture from the mountain appeared. It was of the sunset. She could still picture it. Such a beautiful evening that had ended so tragically.

Poor Conrad. The memory loomed in her mind and her heart broke for the hundredth time.

Before the melancholy thoughts could take over, she moved on to the next photos. Finally one from the overlook came into view. The panoramic picture of the camp. Late-May dusk hovered over the scene, backlit by the last remnants of the glowing sunset.

Kylie double clicked on the edit-picture button on the right column of the screen. She enlarged the photo and lightened it. Squinting one eye, she zeroed in on the two-story cabin. It was a short walk from the girls' cottages, nestled in the pine trees and nearly camouflaged by the stand of evergreens except for a patch of yard beyond the back deck.

And in that small field, a figure appeared. She clicked the mouse to enlarge again. Her mouth gaped.

It was a man, carrying something.

Frantically she clicked the mouse over and over, trying to enlarge the picture enough to see who it was. The little figure grew larger, but the clarity was lost.

Huffing a sigh, she reduced the size a bit and

then flung open the desk drawer. She dug around and located a magnifying glass.

Holding it to the screen, she leaned in and squinted again. She made out the man's thick physique, the black cowboy hat on his head and a plaid shirt as he carried something in his arms. *Someone?*

Dropping the magnifier, Kylie fell back in her seat, holding her chest. Her heart constricted so tightly she wasn't sure it would ever pump normally again. Only one person at camp had dressed like that. And it had to be Conrad he was carrying.

Disbelief barbed through her, making her shudder. How could he do such a thing!

With that question still assailing her, she caught a movement from the corner of her eye. She whipped her head around to the door. It stood ajar. Her gaze tunneled through the open space and down the short hall to the living room. There was nothing.

Kylie got to her feet. A sinking feeling hit the pit of her stomach. She needed to inform Nick about what she'd found. She quickly headed into the living room to retrieve her cell phone.

As she jogged around the corner, she abruptly halted, so fast she almost lost her balance. She grabbed a chair and righted herself, her breath catching as she stared at the man who stood a few yards away, just inside the front door.

His icy green eyes firmly locked on hers as he returned her stare.

"Good afternoon, Kylie." His dry tone revealed even more than the coldness in his eyes. He was there for her.

"Dave." She breathed only the one word.

Nick placed the heated bowl of soup in front of Steven. "What else can I do before I take off?"

"Not a thing. Nadine will be here soon."

Good. Nick was already running later than he planned. He sat down across from Steven and stepped into his boots.

Steven dipped his spoon into the bowl. "If Kylie locates the photos you asked her about, what do you expect she'll find?"

Nick finished tying his shoelaces and sat up. "Maybe nothing, but you never know where hidden treasure lurks."

"True." Steven smacked his lips. "Wow. This soup is hot."

Nick's lack of culinary skills rose to the surface. "I guess eight minutes in the microwave is too much."

"Yeah. By about six minutes."

"Good info. I'll remember that." Nick chuckled and got to his feet. He glanced at the yearbook still on the table. He flipped to page eighty-three. He ran his eyes across the faces one last time.

"Nick, we have company."

Nick's head snapped up. Through the kitchen window, he watched two police cars pull into the driveway. This was getting serious.

He glanced at the yearbook picture again, his gaze landing on Dave Michelson's picture. His crooked smirk. His placid eyes.

Jaw clenching, Nick shot another look out the window. Four officers stepped out of patrol cars. He knew none of them. Dave was the chief investigative detective. He ran the department and had worked elbow to elbow with Nick on the case. Where was he now?

Nick's mind was reeling. Dave had shared information with him, more than he needed to, and now he was out to get Nick. *Interesting.*

Ice poured through his veins. His thoughts came to a screeching halt as the pieces fell into place.

It was Dave.

He grabbed his cell phone and punched Kylie's number.

"Steven, take your time getting to the door. Stall them, tell them whatever you want," he said, holding the phone to his ear and heading toward the basement stairs.

"What's going on?"

"I think Dave Michelson is the culprit. And whatever he has planned, he wants me out of the way."

"How are you going to get out of here without them knowing?" Steven called after him.

"Back road, buddy. For once your cycle will come in handy."

Nick bounded down the basement steps, the phone still to his ear. Kylie wasn't answering. Something was wrong.

A punch of adrenaline rocked through him. He slipped out through the basement door. Staying low and close to the outside wall, he tramped through the overgrown weeds shooting out from cracked ground by the foundation.

At the corner of the house, he hazarded a glance to the four officers waiting for Steven to open the door.

*Good job, brother.*

With measured steps, Nick made his way across the rocky ground to the side of garage. He was grateful he hadn't pulled the bike inside. Maybe God was looking out for him. That thought brought some peace.

With his boot, he eased up the kickstand, then silently pushed the motorcycle back into the woods behind the house. Out of earshot, he jumped on the bike and took off across the rocky terrain. Fifteen minutes to Kylie. *Lord, protect her!*

# NINETEEN

The crazed look in Dave's eyes kept Kylie rooted in place. "What do you want, Dave?"

A slow smirk inched across his jaw. "You, Kylie. That's all I've ever wanted."

Stunned and disbelieving, Kylie grappled for her voice. "Dave, I had no idea you felt that way about me."

Garbled laughter rumbled from his chest. "You knew, Kylie. You just chose not to acknowledge the truth." His assumption shocked her more, jarring intrusively in her ears.

Her knees shaking, Kylie reached for a semblance of composure. She needed to stay calm. In a single glance she gauged the distance between her and the kitchen, wondering if she stood a chance of making it there and out the side door. Then she remembered the new dead bolt she'd recently installed. The key was on her key ring along with the canister of pepper spray Nick had given her.

Her heart slipped, but she kept her chin up. "What truth are you referring to, Dave?"

With a smug tilt to his head, Dave grinned again. "That you and I were meant to be together, of course."

Now Kylie was completely dumbfounded. Her mouth fell open. "How could you think that?" The moment the words tumbled off her tongue, she wished them back.

Dave's features hardened. "For the last ten years I've been in the background of your life. If you had paid attention, you would have noticed." He advanced one step. The anger that lit in his eyes coiled a knot in Kylie's stomach.

She swallowed thickly. "Over the years I've seen you at various functions in town and at church. I would have never guessed that you were there because of me."

His expression eased some. After a pause, he responded, "I knew Nick had hurt you. I was waiting until the timing was right and I thought that time was getting close. But then," he strongly enunciated, "I had Nick to contend with again. I got rid of him once, but as it turned out, not for good. The man couldn't stay away."

Pressing a hand to her throat, Kylie worked to stay calm. She met Dave's intense gaze to hold his attention. Keep him talking. She was buying minutes. "Nick came back to help his brother after the accident."

"No!" Dave's brow furrowed and he wagged his head. "That was only his excuse to sneak back into your life."

Kylie's jaw dropped at the fabrication. Only an obsessive mind would jump to such a conclusion.

"I want you to understand how conniving Nick Bentley is." Dave moved another step in her direction. Fear detonated in her chest.

Fighting to even breathe, Kylie managed a weak nod, encouraging him to keep talking. *Lord, please get Nick here before it's too late.*

"Do you realize how hard I worked to orchestrate such a perfect plan?" Some steel in Dave's voice now. He lifted a clenched fist. "A body at the airport to mark Nick's arrival and when I found out you planned to be there also, the plot turned flawless. I thought for certain that Nick would turn and run at the sight of the first slaughtered victim, like he had after Conrad's murder. I wanted you to see the kind of man he was so you could move on once and for all."

Kylie felt her body stiffen. And fall into Dave's arms? He was crazy.

Dave shook his head. "I would have been there for you, Kylie. I've been waiting patiently all this time."

The puzzle pieces started to match up. Fear bubbled up in Kylie's chest, and to stave off the panic, she kept reminding herself Nick should be arriving any moment.

"I had no idea you cared so much," Kylie finally said.

"Because you only wanted Nick!" he shrieked before his voice softened. "Now that he's back, he's all you think about."

"That's not true." Kylie swallowed. "Nick was just trying to help me. We're friends."

"No!" Dave's distorted expression made her jump. He strode even closer, jabbing a stubby finger at her face. "You couldn't stay away from him. How could I trust you again?"

Kylie threw up her palm. "You can trust me." Her body tensed; her gaze flicked between Dave and the window, praying to see Nick rushing up.

As if Dave could read her mind, he broke into a cynical laugh. "If you're looking for Bentley, you can forget it. He won't be coming."

That brought her gaze back to him in a hurry. "Why would you say that?"

"About now—" Dave twisted his thick wrist and checked his watch "—Nick should be at the station, getting booked and fingerprinted."

Kylie swallowed again, fear clenching her gut. Her brain scrambled for words to defuse him, to gain his trust. Thoughts raced wildly; she snatched one. "It doesn't matter if Nick doesn't come. It's actually better that way."

His brow furrowed, he looked amused. "Why is that, Kylie?"

"Well," she said, stepping back and bumping against the doorjamb, "I wouldn't want him to get hurt on my account."

"He will be hurt," Dave rasped, smiling at her. "Mark my words."

It took a moment for Dave's words to sink in.

He had plans for Nick. Like he had plans for her. Clenching her fists, she stared at him, stared into the eyes of her stalker. Psychopathic eyes. A serial murderer. Her heart lurched. *God, help me!*

He was going to kill her.

"Kylie, I had so hoped for a future for us. But now it seems all you want is Nick. I hate it has to end like this." He continued toward her. She noticed a latex glove jutting from his pocket. "After today, there will be another unsolved murder in Asheville. Too bad you won't be around to report on it."

Fear washed away any thread of composure she had left. She had to get away from him. Even if she couldn't make it out of the house, she needed something to protect herself.

Without a second thought, she broke into a run, daring only one glance back as she rushed for the kitchen. Dave lunged after her, the thud of his boots beating against the polished hardwood.

Yanking a chair from the table, she sent it skidding across the floor, slamming into him.

Cursing and screaming, Dave kicked the chair aside. "Kylie, you're making this difficult!"

*Good.* She reached for the cast-iron skillet on the stove, her fingers tightening around the handle.

Dave's hard hand grabbed her by the arm, yanking her away and sending her stumbling back against his chest. The force of the impact knocked air from her lungs.

His brawny arms tightened around her. "They always run first," he grunted, pressing his lips against her ear. "But they never win."

That knowledge only made her fight harder. She didn't want to end up like one of *them.* Struggling to breathe, she wrenched wildly, trying to break his hold. "Dave, don't do this." She gave a hoarse shriek.

"Stop fighting!" he demanded, his tone gritty. As his grip eased up a fraction, she lobbed an elbow into his ribs.

He growled and she screamed, "Let me go!" Her cry was quickly abated by his crushing hold.

"That's enough." He jerked her up, hugging her small frame against his body, her feet suspended off the floor. Adrenaline kicked up her heart rate and spurred her on. Gulping for air, she kicked frantically and dug her heel into his shin.

"Ouch!" he groaned, releasing his grip. She tumbled to the floor. She fell against the kitchen cabinet, her legs like rubber as she started to stand.

He hauled her up to a full upright position, then whirled her back to him. "Don't play like this, Kylie. You'll only make things worse." Hot breath poured down her neck, sending chills rippling along her skin. Worse didn't seem possible.

"Please stop, Dave." She bucked and squirmed against him as he dragged her across the kitchen, the heels of her shoes dancing along the wood floor.

Halfway across the room, he halted, propped

his hip against the table edge, and with her still locked in his embrace, he managed to extract the gloves from his pocket.

"I never wanted it to come to this. I had such nice plans for us."

"Plans? Tell me about them." She struggled to speak around the lump of fear in her windpipe.

"None of that matters anymore," Dave snarled, wrestling his hand into one of the surgical gloves. "Ten years ago, Nick Bentley was supposed to die. Instead he let Conrad die instead, while he went tromping through the forest with you. If only he'd been where he was supposed to be, none of this would have happened."

So it was Nick he'd wanted all along. Dread gnawed at Kylie's stomach. If Nick had been with Conrad that night, Dave would have killed him, too.

Dave's grip tightened, hugging her closer, making it difficult to breathe. Kylie stilled for a moment, hoping he'd let up some. "Tell me the plans you had for us," she gasped, trying to change his focus to something other than killing her.

"I told you, it's too late for that. You've already crossed the line with Nick. Again!" His tone edged sharper with each spoken word.

As Dave battled with the second glove, his grip relaxed enough for Kylie to take a breath. This was her chance. Gritting her teeth, she slammed her head back into Dave's chin. Before his ragged groan hit her eardrums, she broke away from him and took off for the front door.

To her horror, Dave beat her there, blocking her way. "Kylie, my sweet Kylie." He shook his head, his breathing rapid. "You need to stop this."

*Not on your life.* She grabbed a lamp off a table, her breathing coming in short spurts. Shuffling back, she created more distance between them. She needed to wear him out or somehow convince him to come to his senses.

"Dave, you don't have to do this." She held the lamp above her head as endless prayers raced through her mind.

Slow and calculated, Dave snapped his gloves into place. Giving her a cynical look, he moved across the floor, his cold green eyes fixed on her. "Drop the lamp, Kylie."

Fear coiled more tightly inside her with each step he took, followed by a shudder that shook her whole body. Clutching the lamp in a death grip, she continued to hold her ground, continued to pray, worked to breathe.

"I wanted to make this simple, Kylie." Dave's voice broke. But his flat tone bore an edge of impatience, sending dread coursing through her veins. "Unfortunately, you've given me no choice."

Kylie's breath snagged as Dave hunched his shoulders and broke into a sprint, rushing at her like a defensive linebacker.

She let go of the lamp, sending it crashing onto

the floor, glass shards scattering. Spinning on her heel, she tore across the room, but Dave gained on her quickly, and in one clumsy tackle he took her to the floor.

"It's time for you to give up, Kylie," he grunted, his husky frame pinning her to the ground.

Fortunately, willpower trumped exhaustion. Kylie relentlessly twisted and writhed beneath him, and somewhere between a sob and a prayer, she managed to wrestle one arm free to scratch his face.

With a snarl, Dave knocked her hand away, then grabbed her throat and started squeezing.

"Dave, please don—" she gasped. A loud thud drowned out the rest of her words. Then a crash as the front door burst open.

Nick's shout rumbled like an avalanche. "Kylie!"

Unable to answer, Kylie thrashed about, struggling to breathe and working to dislodge Dave's fingers from her neck, but he grasped harder.

As Nick bolted into the room, Dave sprang up and in one jerky movement he was on his feet, dragging Kylie with him. He wrenched her in front of him, clutching his arm around her waist. He fumbled in the pocket of his jacket and pulled out a knife. He thrust the steel blade against her throat.

Kylie's heart thrummed against her sternum.

Nick's steps ground to a halt. Out of habit, he surveyed the scene, but his eyes kept going back to the knife at Kylie's throat. "Let her go, Dave." He started to raise his arms, a gesture of surrender and to show he had no weapon.

Dave didn't budge, but the blade of his knife pressed more firmly to Kylie's jugular. "One step, Nick," he growled, "and she's dead. Remember, I'm good at this."

As if he could forget. Nick nodded, lowered his hands. His gaze moved from the knife to Kylie's eyes.

She stared back at him; a fat tear spilled onto her cheek.

A desperate plan started to form in Nick's head. "It's your game, Dave. What do you want from us?" Nick lowered his hands and took a tentative step.

"I'm not kidding, Bentley!" Dave shuffled back a bit, dragging Kylie with him.

Cringing, Kylie's gaze went wide.

"Dave, I believe you," Nick said, shooting one hand up again. "Just tell me what you want from me."

"I want you dead, Bentley!" Dave spat. He pulled Kylie tighter, terror etched her fine features.

Nick's jaw tightened. "Okay, Dave. Let Kylie go and you can go at it with me. You have a knife. I'm unarmed. It's more than fair."

A cynical laugh escaped him. "I don't need to prove anything to you, Bentley. I have everything I need to hurt you right here."

That fact scared Nick to death. "This isn't about Kylie, is it? It's about us."

Dave bobbed his head as madness gleamed in his eyes and a hint of a grimace curled his thin lips. "You've taken everything from me. You are the reason I have to kill. The reason I can't have Kylie."

As Nick glared at Dave, he watched his every move. The way his teeth clenched, the way his hand trembled, the knife quavering at Kylie's neck. Dave's composure was starting to shred. One wrong move and Nick would be ready.

"Dave, you misunderstood my intentions with Kylie. So let go of her and we'll talk."

"Do you think I'm crazy?" Dave roared and Nick held his tongue. He wasn't about to answer that. "We have nothing to talk about. You've already ruined my life!"

"I've ruined your life?" Nick kept his voice calm and his eyes locked on Dave's.

"You absolutely have!" Dave pointed his knife at Nick.

Those were the few seconds of opportunity that Nick needed. He broke eye contact with Dave and quickly gestured with a flick of his head for Kylie to get out of there.

As Kylie shot out of Dave's grip, Nick lunged forward and threw a straight left kick, knocking the knife from Dave's hand.

Dave's growl lit the air as he whirled around and

charged at him. Jumping back, Nick swung his leg over Dave's head, sending him into the back of a chair. Dave nearly tumbled to his knees, but regaining his footing, he turned, a bloody gash over his eye, and came at Nick with a right hook. "Are you going to kill me, Nick? Do it! You'll be no better than me!"

There had been enough killing. With a groan, Nick shielded himself and grabbed Dave's arm, flipping him over his shoulder. Dave landed with a thud. "Give it up, Dave. We've both had enough."

Back on his feet, Dave huffed, "I'm not finished with you, Bentley." He clumsily danced around as if he was trying to gain momentum, then lunged at Nick, grabbing for his neck.

Nick's heart rate spiked as he thrust a palm into Dave's chest. Latching on to Nick's shirt, Dave stumbled back, ripping the fabric and sending buttons flying.

Nick readied himself. Although Dave was no match for him, he'd let him exhaust himself.

Regaining his balance, Dave came at him again, but Nick jumped in the air, spun around and pummeled him in the abdomen with a flying left kick, sending him slamming into the wall.

"I'm…going to…kill…you…Nick." Hyperventilating, Dave went to his knees.

*Okay. Done.* Hunkering down, Nick secured Dave's wrists behind his back. Then, giving a cursory glance around, he spotted Kylie standing in the kitchen doorway. She was gaping slightly, eyebrows tentatively raised, and gripping an iron skillet in her hand.

Resourceful. He liked that.

"Ky, are you okay?"

She nodded. "I am now."

"Could you grab some duct tape? And if you haven't called the cops yet, that would nice." He winked and was pleased when she smiled.

She lowered the pan. "They're already on the way."

Got to love that girl. And he did.

Thirty minutes later, Kylie clung to Nick, feeling safe in his embrace as they stood on her front porch and watched two officers wrestle Detective Dave Michelson into the backseat of a police cruiser.

The nightmare was over. The mystery of Conrad Miller's death was finally solved. Tears of relief stung Kylie's eyes. *Thank You, Lord, for getting us through this.*

"I think I've got everything I need." The older police sergeant pocketed his notepad.

"You have my number if you think of any other questions," Nick said, tightening his grip on Kylie. "We'd like to see Dave tried and convicted in short order."

"I understand." The officer nodded. "The whole town will be glad to put this ordeal behind them.

With the charges facing Michelson—four counts of murder, two counts of attempted murder and a stalking charge—he'll be locked up for a long, long time."

"Good to hear," Kylie and Nick said in unison.

As the sergeant walked away, Kylie twisted out of Nick's arms. She looked up at him. "So what now, Captain Bentley?"

A smile curved his generous lips. "Well, I've recently had a bit of a revelation."

"Really?" Kylie looked at him more intently. "What kind of a revelation?"

"I realized how much I lost when I left ten years ago. My home, my faith and my heart. And the hurt I caused you because of those choices is my greatest regret."

She fluttered her lashes. "What does all that mean?"

"It means I no longer want to live a life of regrets."

A trickle of hope snaked into her heart, but she held it at bay. She swallowed. "Then don't leave Asheville again."

"And if I stay?" He gave her a questioning look.

Kylie shook her head, convinced that he wasn't serious. "Don't play with my emotions, please."

"All right." Nick extended his hand. "Let's do this right."

For a moment she couldn't breathe. "What?"

"Come on." He canted his head and captured

her hand. In one steady movement she was in his arms.

She gulped a breath and her heart melted at the hope in his eyes. She almost requested that he pinch her, to make sure this wasn't a dream. Because if this wasn't real, her heart was history.

His arms tightened around her. Not a pinch, but good enough. She sighed.

"Are you okay?"

Kylie nodded. *Very much okay,* she wanted to say, but she couldn't speak for the lump in her throat.

She glimpsed the thoughtful expression crossing his features, and she could almost feel his hesitation. Then he smiled, a slow, crooked smile that warmed her deeply.

"Kylie Harper, I'll ask you again. What happens if I stay?"

She closed her eyes, scarcely believing. "A new life between us, I suppose."

"You suppose?"

She flinched and opened her eyes. "I hope."

He arched a dark brow. "Only hope?"

"I know," she whispered.

He leaned closer to kiss the tip of her nose. "Sold."

Nearly blinded by the tears in her eyes, she curled a hand over the nape of his neck. "I'm going to hold you to this."

"Promise?" That crooked smile again.

"Promise."

Pressing his forehead against hers, he stared intently into her eyes. "Forever?"

"Forever," she whispered before he kissed her, his lips gentle against hers. And their love, kept at bay for so long, blossomed, deepening their kiss and flooding passion into their souls.

# TWENTY

*Six months later*

There was good-size turnout. Nick counted about two hundred people gathered by the front steps of the Asheville Municipal Building.

Mayor Delbert Carlisle stepped up to the microphone. "It is my pleasure to extend congratulations to Captain Nicholas Bentley following his election as police and crime commissioner for the city of Asheville and Buncombe County."

The crowd burst into applause.

Mayor Carlisle held up a hand. "Let me just share some of our incoming commissioner's accomplishments. As a veteran of the United States Army, Captain Bentley was part of a Delta Force special-operations unit. As an elite Special Forces soldier, he was involved in covert missions..."

Standing off to the side and out of spectator view, Nick leaned in and slipped his arm around Kylie. "I already don't like this part of my job."

Kylie cast him a sidelong glance. "What part?" she whispered.

"Public speaking. I'm more of a behind-the-scenes, hunt-down-the-criminal kind of guy. Politics and pomp are not my thing. And this suit—" Nick pulled at the collar "—definitely not me."

"Should I be surprised by this revelation?" Kylie picked a piece of lint from his jacket.

Nick laughed when he saw her teasing smile. "So you won't mind if we skip out early from the mayor's banquet today?"

"Well," Kylie said, giving a slight shrug, "the dinner's in your honor, but if you don't want to stay long and mingle, I guess that's fine."

Nick bent in a little closer. "I have plans tonight that I can't break."

Pulling back, Kylie blinked up at him. "Really? Do I know about these plans?"

"Actually—" Nick glanced right and left and then winked. "It's a surprise for my wife."

A killer smile crossed her face, the one that sent his heart into palpitations. "A surprise, you say?" Kylie nuzzled up to him.

"Yes." He brushed a kiss against her temple. "I'll give you a little hint. A cozy cabin in the woods, three dozen yellow roses…"

"Oh, my, three dozen yellow roses?" She pulled back slightly, flicking a glance at him.

"In celebration of our three-month anniversary." Kylie melted against him again.

Marriage was definitely working for him.

"Citizens of Asheville, let's welcome Commissioner Nick Bentley to the stage!" The mayor's introduction was followed by more applause.

Nick snapped back into commissioner mode. "Come on." He grabbed Kylie's hand and they started walking.

"I don't think I'm supposed go on stage with you."

Nick glanced at his wife before he stepped into public view. "Ky, I want you by my side now and forever."

And the smile she sent him told him that was exactly where she wanted to be.

Now and forever.

\* \* \* \* \*

Dear Reader,

I hope you enjoyed reading about Nick and Kylie in *Smoky Mountain Investigation*. Their story is built around lost love, forgiveness and trust. By pushing aside guilt, forgiveness and trust are possible and by God's grace they are able to move on together in love.

Nestled between the scenic Blue Ridge and the Great Smoky Mountains of North Carolina, Asheville's abundant natural beauty and great quality of life made a beautiful setting for the story to evolve. Although street names and names of establishments visited by the characters are fictional, the lush forests and rich mountain setting play an integral part of the story.

Life isn't always easy and rarely goes as planned. Many things happen we don't understand. But there is one constant in our world that never changes: the living God. It blesses me to know that by His grace anything is possible.

May you find His blessings in all you do,
*Annslee Urban*

# Questions for Discussion

1. Why did you decide to read this book? Was the story appealing to you?

2. Were the memories Nick and Kylie shared from their past clear to you? Was the tragedy that happened at camp believable?

3. Did you find Nick's and Kylie's characters likable and believable?

4. As the story evolved, did the suspense keep you turning the pages?

5. Did you enjoy the pace at which the romance built between Nick and Kylie?

6. Nick held on to the guilt of his friend Conrad's death. How did forgiving himself impact the story? What happens when we carry guilt?

7. Detective Dave loved Kylie from afar. Why did he finally decide that he needed to kill her?

8. Horrific memories left Nick with a sour taste for a city he once loved. What happens when someone forgets the good memories and focuses on the bad?

9. Did you enjoy the Scripture at the beginning of the book? What do you think God is telling us? How does it apply to your life?

10. Nick left behind the woman he loved to escape the pain and guilt he felt after his friend was murdered. What happens when we run away from our problems instead of addressing them?

11. Did you enjoy the author's writing style and pace of the story?

12. What life lessons can you take away from Nick and Kylie's story?

# LARGER-PRINT BOOKS!

## GET 2 FREE
## LARGER-PRINT NOVELS
## PLUS 2 FREE
## MYSTERY GIFTS

*Love Inspired*

### Larger-print novels are now available...

**YES!** Please send me 2 FREE LARGER-PRINT Love Inspired® novels and my 2 FREE mystery gifts (gifts are worth about $10). After receiving them, if I don't wish to receive any more books, I can return the shipping statement marked "cancel." If I don't cancel, I will receive 6 brand-new novels every month and be billed just $5.24 per book in the U.S. or $5.74 per book in Canada. That's a savings of at least 23% off the cover price. It's quite a bargain! Shipping and handling is just 50¢ per book in the U.S. and 75¢ per book in Canada.* I understand that accepting the 2 free books and gifts places me under no obligation to buy anything. I can always return a shipment and cancel at any time. Even if I never buy another book, the two free books and gifts are mine to keep forever.

122/322 IDN F49Y

| | | |
|---|---|---|
| Name | (PLEASE PRINT) | |
| Address | | Apt. # |
| City | State/Prov. | Zip/Postal Code |

Signature (if under 18, a parent or guardian must sign)

Mail to the **Harlequin® Reader Service:**
**IN U.S.A.:** P.O. Box 1867, Buffalo, NY 14240-1867
**IN CANADA:** P.O. Box 609, Fort Erie, Ontario L2A 5X3

**Are you a current subscriber to Love Inspired books
and want to receive the larger-print edition?
Call 1-800-873-8635 or visit www.ReaderService.com.**

* Terms and prices subject to change without notice. Prices do not include applicable taxes. Sales tax applicable in N.Y. Canadian residents will be charged applicable taxes. Offer not valid in Quebec. This offer is limited to one order per household. Not valid for current subscribers to Love Inspired Larger-Print books. All orders subject to credit approval. Credit or debit balances in a customer's account(s) may be offset by any other outstanding balance owed by or to the customer. Please allow 4 to 6 weeks for delivery. Offer available while quantities last.

**Your Privacy**—The Harlequin® Reader Service is committed to protecting your privacy. Our Privacy Policy is available online at www.ReaderService.com or upon request from the Harlequin Reader Service.

We make a portion of our mailing list available to reputable third parties that offer products we believe may interest you. If you prefer that we not exchange your name with third parties, or if you wish to clarify or modify your communication preferences, please visit us at www.ReaderService.com/consumerchoice or write to us at Harlequin Reader Service Preference Service, P.O. Box 9062, Buffalo, NY 14269. Include your complete name and address.

LILPDIR13R

# *Reader Service*.com

## Manage your account online!
- Review your order history
- Manage your payments
- Update your address

***We've designed
the Harlequin® Reader Service
website just for you.***

## Enjoy all the features!
- Reader excerpts from any series
- Respond to mailings and
  special monthly offers
- Discover new series available to you
- Browse the Bonus Bucks catalog
- Share your feedback

*Visit us at:*

**ReaderService.com**

RS13